Some WOMEN DON'T PLAY *by the* RULES

A DUET OF FEISTY WOMEN

ALYSSA ALEXANDER

To Joe
My rock and hero. Thanks for putting up with this feisty woman.

To Josh
You make every day an adventure. Thanks for sometimes still thinking
I'm cool.

ACKNOWLEDGMENTS

Although the general view of writing is that it's a solitary endeavor, it is not true. No writer is truly alone. Whether it is agent, editor, spouse, friend, critique partner, or writing groups, no one writes a book alone. If we did, it would be *awful.* But the truth is, while writing seems like a lonely occupation and often is, there are always people who help us along the way.

To the ladies of the Dukes by the Dozen and A Midsummer Night's Romance anthologies in which these original novellas appeared, and most specifically Anna Harrington, I owe you so much! From grammar to plotting to sharing the joy of hitting the USA Today Bestseller's List. I heart you all!

To Gina, for your enthusiastic plotting. You always ask the hard questions, which result in me going, huh. I dunno why she is doing that. You make me think, and I love it.

To Meika, not only did you read my pages, but you did so while writing your own. I am delighted and privileged to know you and write with you, sometimes online and sometimes in person (Covid and all that). You inspire me. I am so lucky to call you a friend!

Christina, THANK YOU for the cover and formatting. Because, erm, I'm so not savvy in that way. Websites? Sure. Covers? No. I couldn't have done this without you! Thanks for holding my hand and all your sage advice.

And as always, to the Mid-Michigan Romance Writers of America chapter, a group of fabulous, caring, wonderful women who have supported me in so many ways during the last decade-plus I have been part of the group. I wouldn't be where I am without you!

Duke in Winter

One

January 1802
An English Country House

"**B**eatrice," came the inebriated drawl. "Don't be a prude."

"Of course not." There was a great deal of difference between prude and debauched, and Bea was decidedly in the middle.

Despite not being a prude, Lady Beatrice Falk wrinkled her nose, shifting the spectacles perched there. The scent of liquor in the room was strong enough it seemed a snifter had been waved beneath her nose. Or someone had bathed in brandy.

"If you are not here to scold, then let me be." An empty decanter winked at Bea from the side table, just as her brother winked at her from his position on the chaise longue. He sprawled over the cushions, cravat loose, the buttons of his coat and waistcoat open to reveal his shirt beneath. He raised his glass, gestured vaguely at the room in general. "It's a lovely time here, Sister, even if you won't partake."

"Lovely," she repeated, eyeing the tableau before her.

Dice rolled between the shadows and firelight, and in one corner cards *shushed* against each other. Low laughter and murmurs floated between curls of tobacco smoke, swirled around bare feminine shoulders and rouged cheeks.

Bea quickly counted heads. As she'd believed, three gentlemen were missing. Some of her quarry were drunk on the drawing room floor and were of no use that evening, but others would be making their way through frozen trees to their own country homes.

She'd best get moving.

Still, she was mistress of the house until her brother married, and with that came responsibilities. *Someone* had to attend to them.

"I've instructed the butler to ensure your remaining guests have beds this night." Bea pushed her spectacles up her nose. "Stewart has spoken with the housekeeper, who will see to it."

"Excellent." Her brother half-stood, raising his glass in an enthusiastic salute. As he listed to one side, gold liquid sloshed over the rim, dripping down his already soiled evening glove. He frowned, studying the newest stain. "Damn."

A triumphant burst of sound rose from one side of the room. Bea watched money change hands over dice—so much money, with no purpose but gambling and drink. And perhaps to pay the laughing women standing beside the players. A pretty lot of courtesans made garish by rouge and paint and revealing gowns.

"Well, now. I think this requires a proper celebration." The winner staggered to his feet, puffing out his chest so the embroidery on his waistcoat rippled with the strain.

Sir Winthrop. A close friend of her brother's, the man had asked for her hand three times the year of her debut. When it was clear she would remain a spinster, he'd twice suggested they be lovers.

Unlike her brother, Bea chose her lovers with great care—and marriage was out of the question with the life she led.

With a leer at one of the girls that jiggled the whiskers on his jowls, Sir Winthrop pointed to his empty glass. "We could call for another bottle. Share it, you know."

The girl giggled through painted red lips and opened her mouth to answer, but Sir Winthrop had turned away and raised the glass high.

"Here! Another bottle!" he called out, plainly searching for a footman—only his gaze landed on Bea. Expression turning sly, he stumbled toward her. "Oh, ho, my lady. Come to play?"

"I do not think so, Sir Winthrop." Bea attempted to keep the revulsion from layering over her voice. "Thank you for your offer. However, I am retiring. Enjoy your evening."

Closing the drawing room doors behind her, Bea strode across the entrance hall and abandoned the guests without a backward glance. They would still be there in the morning, in various stages of drunkenness and disarray.

The men who mattered were those who had left.

With one hand, Bea removed the spectacles she didn't need. With the other, she began to loosen the old wig of long, curling brown hair. Being a spinster of undetermined years buried in the country, no one cared if she still wore unfashionable wigs.

But they suited her purpose.

———

HE'D MISJUDGED THE WEATHER.

Howling wind kicked up the snow already covering the ground, mixing it with heavy, falling flakes. Only thirty minutes before, when Wulf had requested his horse be brought around to the front of Falk Manor, the moon had still been visible between the moving clouds. Now, with the impending snowstorm and the lack of moonlight, Wulf would be fortunate to return home. Ever.

He should have requested a room at Falk Manor, stayed until morning.

Even as he thought it, Wulf grimaced. Old childhood friendships still demanded attention, even though the tradition of a yule log, punch, and country dances had given way to brandy and women once the old earl died.

Now it was dissolution of the most juvenile kind.

Still, the duty was done, and Wulfric Standover, Duke of Highrow, was far enough from the festivities that the disgust clinging to his skin was slipping away.

Hunching his shoulders against the bitter wind, Wulf guided his stallion onto the narrow track between the trees. With luck, he would be standing before his own fire before the storm worsened.

"Stand and deliver!" The shout was sharp beneath the swirling snow, echoing between the silent, naked trees.

Cursing, Wulf lifted his forearm to block the white flakes and studied the shadows dancing between the wind-tossed snow.

The highwayman was not ten feet away, sitting atop a horse in the center of the path. His greatcoat swirled in the wind as he raised his arm, the double-barreled pistol he held appearing small and light.

Though size was not indicative of deadliness. The thief held the weapon as straight and steady as any spymaster Wulf had encountered during the Reign of Terror.

"What shall I deliver?" Wulf pitched his voice above the wind and narrowed his eyes, evaluating risk. He kept a pistol in his saddlebags, but he would never be fast enough to beat his opponent.

Still, he took one hand from the reins and slid it onto his thigh. Easily, he hoped, so it would seem natural and not calculated to move closer to the saddlebags.

"You may deliver whatever valuables you have on your person." Through the eerie, dim, snow-light and thickening flakes, Wulf could distinguish a cap pulled low and a scarf wrapped around the thief's face that was substantial enough to fight the wind. "Beginning with the winnings in your pockets, sir."

"Now, how is it you know about the blunt in my pockets?" Wulf leaned casually on the pommel. Considered his adversary.

"A rich nabob like you, coming from a house party? Of course you have blunt." The man's jacket was big enough he was swimming in it. A local lad, perhaps, fallen on difficult times.

Or the Honorable Highwayman.

Wulf had yet to make the acquaintance of the local legend, though he had heard a great deal about the highwayman's ill-gained generosity.

"I don't particularly care to give up my blunt, even for widows and orphans." Though Wulf was actually quite willing to forgo his winnings for such a cause. "At least not at the end of a pistol," he continued, attempting to stall.

Another few inches and Wulf would be able to reach his weapon. He shifted again, setting his hand a little closer to the saddlebag.

Wind rattled the branches above them, so they clacked and creaked like brittle bones. Wulf's stallion sidestepped, pranced a few paces. Using both hands—unfortunately—Wulf brought the animal under control again.

"Very well, Your Grace." The highwayman's pistol notched higher, its barrels seeming to stare at Wulf with two dark, round eyes. "Then I shall wound you with the first shot. Perhaps you shall change your mind."

"Unlikely." Still, Wulf had lost the precious inches he'd gained reaching for his own weapon. His stallion was edgy, the storm swirled around them—and the coins and pound notes in his pocket were not worth the effort.

But by God, it was the principle. He'd not spent years dodging the guillotine in France only to be bested by a highwayman a few miles from his home.

The wind sharpened, howled, and in the momentary silence as it died again, Wulf clearly heard a long-suffering sigh.

"As you wish, Your Grace."

The pistol's report was deafening, slicing through the silence of snow and night. The already-spooked stallion reared, pawed the air. Even as Wulf recognized the searing pain in his shoulder for what it was, he understood he would not keep his seat.

"Bloody hell!" he cursed, tumbling through flying snow.

When the ground slammed into the back of his head, everything went black.

She'd shot him. Actually shot him.

"Damnation." As the sound of panicked horse hooves faded into the night, Bea looked down at her pistol and let out an irritated huff. "Why did you have to pick *now* to be slippery?"

Her aim was nearly perfect, and she'd never yet wounded any of her intended prey.

Only frightened them.

Bea contemplated the man sprawled on the ground as snow began to blanket his greatcoat. She couldn't leave him here. Unconscious, wounded, and without a horse, since his had gone running off into the trees.

He was also the Duke of Highrow—a boy she'd known. A man she didn't.

"Damnation," she said again, as she saw the stains on the snow. Blood. She didn't need sunlight to recognize the dark drops dotting the ground.

Uncocking the second barrel of her pistol, Bea tucked the weapon into the waist of her breeches and dismounted. She tied her mare's reins to the nearest tree, then strode forward.

Highrow lay on his back, face bared to the dark sky and biting wind.

Crouching, she probed his shoulder among the folds of his greatcoat and evaluated the damage.

He groaned, which was heartening.

Her search revealed the ball had grazed his shoulder and was little more than a flesh wound. Bea repeated the actions on the back of his head, hatless now. Beneath thick hair just long enough to curl over his collar, she found a large knot. It was no wonder he was unconscious.

Shifting, Bea stared down at the duke. She was close enough to discern the lean planes of his cheekbones, the strong jaw. Although she did not need any light to remember he was handsome. Extraordinarily so. Bea had known it since she was old enough to toddle after him at the village fair or at picnics. Before he had been the Duke of Highrow.

He had been *Wulf* to her, then. Especially when he'd grown into a young man who teased and laughed with her, indulging a young girl's foolish infatuation.

Bea swallowed hard as guilt rippled through her. She'd wounded an old friend, even if it was barely a scratch. She ought to feel more appalled than she did, she supposed. But then, a highwayman did not feel pity for their victims when they were entirely too wealthy for their own good. Which he was.

Her bad fortune that Wulf's tracks were the set she'd followed. He had never been her target. If there was one man the Honorable Highwayman knew to avoid, it was Wulfric Standover. He had been a soldier for far too long.

Leaning back on her heels, she studied the prone man. Well, she couldn't leave him here. Wulf wouldn't bleed to death, but he'd certainly freeze.

Bea judged the area, stared up into the driving snow. The storm was getting worse. Blinding. The bite of the wind penetrated her woolen coat and even the thick scarf she'd wrapped about her face.

"I suppose I should take care of you, now I've shot you." Bea shook him a little, careful not to jostle his head, and was rewarded with a groaning curse. "Wake up," she shouted over a sudden, howling gust of wind.

Wulf twitched, cursed again, and clutched his shoulder.

"Easy now," she said, pitching her voice to the lower tenor she used as a highwayman. "I imagine it burns like hell, but it is not bad."

Eyes flicking open, he stared up at her. She remembered quite clearly the deep blue of his irises, though in the night they only appeared to be dark and fathomless.

She wondered briefly if he would recognize her, then dismissed the idea. He'd never recognize her in her current garb. No one ever did. Hair short, no spectacles. Breeches. And it had been nearly a decade since they exchanged more than brief pleasantries. Wulf had been at war, and when he was home, he had paid no attention to an aging spinster.

"Bloody hell, my head hurts." Slowly, as if testing whether his skull would stay attached, Wulf turned to face her more fully.

"I imagine so. You've a knot back there—not caused by me, I am happy to report. That was the ground." Bea fought not to set a comforting hand on the broad expanse of his chest. Drawing back, she met his gaze. "Can you sit? Stand?"

"You *shot* me." Struggling to a sitting position, Wulf peered up at her from beneath hair whipped by the storm into an unruly frenzy. Fury sharpened the already keen planes of his face.

"I told you I would. Now, you are bleeding, and we will both die if we do not find shelter." She pointed to the sky. "Snowstorm."

"Surely, this is a jest. Or a dream."

"Not at all." Bea pushed to standing, careful to keep the scarf hiding her face. "I know of a cottage not far from here. We will be safe enough until the storm lets up."

Another groan, and Wulf staggered to his feet. Casting his gaze about the path, he growled, "Where the devil is my horse?"

"The horse has run off, and I don't think there's much to be done for him." Bea retrieved her own mare, who still stood patiently waiting in the trees. "Horses are wily creatures, though. He'll find a place to weather the— er, weather. As we should do, unless you'd prefer I leave you here to freeze?"

A long, weighty pause spun out, fighting the tossed snowflakes.

"First," he said finally, "you intend to rob me—I presume you're the Honorable Highwayman?" At her short, acknowledging nod, he continued. "Then you shoot me, and now you plan to shelter with me?"

"I won't shoot you again. I give you my word." Bea shrugged, though she sent up a quick prayer he would not recognize her once they reached the cottage. Yet she could not abandon him. "You can't walk back, my horse can't carry the weight of both of us, and you really should attend to the wound. Also, I cannot help being honest. Or at least, to a degree. Leaving you here to freeze seems—dishonest."

He stared at her, mouth open. "What strange hell have I fallen into?"

———

WULF WAS NOT SO foolish as to deny himself refuge from the weather, even if he was sheltering with a daft highwayman.

The little cottage hunkered between dense trees, appearing barely strong enough to withstand the storm. An even more dilapidated shed leaned beside it. Wulf warily eyed the structures, expecting them to blow over at any moment.

Yet the highwayman was correct that weathering the storm overnight would be impossible. Wulf was trapped—no horse and too far from sanctuary, and now he carried no weapon.

Add to that, his damned wounds. Pain burned through Wulf's shoulder—a pain he'd felt before, having taken a musket ball to the thigh in France, another in the shoulder in Brussels. Probing this new injury proved it was only a nick, as the highwayman indicated, and the blood had already thickened and slowed.

It was his aching head he couldn't escape.

The highwayman gestured toward the cottage door, as if shooing Wulf inside. Narrowing his eyes, Wulf watched the man carefully lead his horse toward the shed.

No choice but to enter the cottage. Even if Wulf overpowered the slight man, restrained him, what would that accomplish? Very little at present. So, he would wait and see.

He pushed at the cottage door, but it was stuck tight. Gritting his teeth, he thrust his good shoulder against the worn wood. The movement made his head throb, his abused shoulder beating in time even though he favored it, but he burst into the room with an explosion of dust and snow.

Breath curling out to fade into the dark, Wulf studied the single room and the shadowed furniture ranged throughout. Beyond the walls, the wind shrieked and wailed, but there was no betraying whistle. The cold would not fight its way between the wattle and daub that snugged the cottage frame. The little structure would do well enough.

He picked his way toward the shadow of the wide hearth. Searching blindly with his good arm, he found a tinderbox and stacked wood. Kindling sat neatly beside it.

The cottage might have *appeared* abandoned, but it clearly was not.

He began to build the fire by touch rather than sight, then glanced over as he heard the highwayman step inside. The man moved toward a deep shadow, lifted something. As the kindling caught in the hearth, Wulf saw it was a blanket.

"For the horse," came the explanation. The voice was smooth now that it wasn't fighting the storm and wind. Just how young was the highwayman? "I will return in a moment."

Whatever the highwayman's age, he was no fool. He kept his back to the wall, eyes on Wulf, until he slipped once more through the door and into the storm. Wulf could not fault him.

As the fire grew, the shadowy outlines of furniture became visible. A table and chairs, trunks lining one wall, shelves holding lanterns, crockery—even a teapot. Light crept into the dark, chilled corners of the room just as the highwayman returned.

"A fire. Excellent." He shoved the door closed, blocking out the howling wind and any sense of the world beyond.

"What is this place?" Wulf added more wood, watched it catch and be consumed by flame.

"Only a cottage well-stocked by those who might need it from time to time." Face still partially concealed by the scarf, the highwayman stared at Wulf with eyes deep and dark.

"Criminals? Poachers?" Any number of secrets might be hidden in the shadows of the room.

"Perhaps." A pause, then the deep, dark eyes crinkled at the corners.

"Or a man who has angered his wife and wishes for a temporary roof over his head."

"That would explain the blankets and crockery." There were such places in the forests in every country of the world. Espionage occurred in many of them.

"A man needs to eat and sleep, even if his wife disagrees." The highwayman stepped into the ring of firelight and held out gloved hands for warmth.

Wulf watched his opponent, examining the man who had shot him. He moved with a strange type of grace, held his slight shoulders stiffly beneath the greatcoat. The bottom of his face was still covered, but the delicate line of a nose and narrow, curved brows were discernable.

A thought began to form, as if all Wulf had needed was to organize the pieces of information he knew into the proper shape. Shock arrowed through him, swift and forceful, but he knew the truth.

"You are a woman."

"No." The highwayman did not look up, instead keeping his—*her* —face toward the fire.

"The small mare, the movement of your body, your voice, even the tea pot there on the shelf—it is clear enough, if a man looks close." And Wulf always looked, because he had learned long ago that details could keep a spy alive. "You are a woman."

There was a lengthy pause, as if the highwayman was weighing the benefits of the admitting the truth.

"Very well, Highrow." She began to unwind the scarf, slowly and deliberately, features beginning to emerge. A lush mouth. Creamy skin pinked by the cold. Large, thickly-lashed eyes. The scarf fell to the floor and her cap followed suit, revealing short, sweetly curling hair.

She watched him for a moment, as if waiting for something significant.

"Is that all? Any other secrets?" After being shot, forced into sheltering with his adversary, and discovering she was a woman, Wulf wasn't certain he could withstand any other shocks.

"I think that should do it." She crouched in front of the hearth, pulling off her gloves and reaching toward the heat with elegant hands. Gold light edged over high cheekbones, over the strong curve of her jaw.

He must be dreaming. Perhaps he'd had too much brandy at the house party after all.

Except his shoulder burned and his head throbbed. The wind howled beyond the cottage door, rattling the windowpanes in their frames. Heat burgeoned from the flames well on their way to a blaze.

This was no dream.

The Honorable Highwayman was a woman. Clad in scarred leather boots and thick buckskin breeches, swallowed by the heavy greatcoat, but clearly a woman.

Wulf had never heard a whisper of such rumors.

Even as the revelation sank in, he searched her features for recognition, but could not recall seeing that strong face before.

The woman pushed to her feet. Angling her head to meet his gaze while loose curls danced around her face, she said softly, "I *am* sorry I shot you."

Three

"I usually miss after the warning—on purpose," she added slyly. "My aim is quite accurate. Tonight the pistol slipped a little, 'tis all."

"Forgive me if I am not impressed by your skill." Confusion did not sit well on his shoulders, so Wulf shuffled what he knew of the Honest Highwayman to meet this new version of the truth. "I suppose I should thank you for not leaving me to freeze after you shot me."

"So you should, though that is neither here nor there at the moment. There are more important matters." She raised a brow, almost as if challenging him to disagree. "Please remove your greatcoat."

"In order for you to inspect your handiwork?"

Wulf had forgotten the pain in the midst of his surprise, but it flooded back now with a hot burst. Burning his shoulder, beating against his skull.

"Just so." Slim fingers began to efficiently unbutton her own great-coat, moving swiftly over the wool.

He was not certain he trusted his eyes as the outer garment fell to the floor. It was considerably smaller than his own, yet with its capes and squared shoulders it was no less masculine.

The body beneath was anything but.

Curved. Every bit of her was curved. Not lean or slender, or trying to hide in the breeches and coat. Instead, she was boldly feminine, the male clothing emphasizing every contour of hip and waist and breast.

His mouth went dry.

She did not notice. Instead, she ran her hand through loose, gold-brown curls, shaking her head as if to free them from an invisible band. "Please, come close to the fire so I may see the wound," she commanded. As she angled her head, considering him, she murmured, "How is your head?"

Throbbing in tandem with other body parts.

"Well enough," he said curtly, moving closer to the hearth as its building heat echoed the building heat in his blood. "I suppose if you shot me, you should attend to the wound."

Despite his head, despite the arm held stiffly against his side, a visceral, unexpected need gripped him. Clawed at his gut. Wulf wanted to understand this woman, unravel the mystery of her as he might a code from Napoleon's spies. Unwrap each layer and discover what lay hidden beneath both her clothing and her unusual pursuits.

A woman taking to the road as a highwayman was interesting, indeed.

"I will bring a chair over while you remove your greatcoat." She nodded toward a pair of simple chairs huddled beside the table. "You are so tall, I shan't be able to reach your shoulder properly unless you are sitting."

"I am not so feeble as to be unable to retrieve a simple wooden chair." With his good arm, Wulf picked up the nearest chair and set it carefully on the floor beside the hearth.

"Men." She shook her head and laughed, the sound husky and amused—and very much in keeping with her accompanying half-smile. "I suppose I have already stung your pride by shooting you."

"Quite." Carefully, Wulf began to unbutton his greatcoat. After dropping it to the floor, he set to work on the jacket. Gritting his teeth, he slowly eased it off until he stood only in his waistcoat and shirtsleeves.

Blood liberally stained the sleeve of his shirt, brilliant crimson against stunning white.

"Oh, God." Her whispered words held quiet distress. Full lips pressed together, thinned, then parted again after a deep inhale. "Hell, Highrow. I truly am sorry."

"So I see." Wulf settled gingerly in the chair, quite certain of her regret.

"I did not think there would be so much blood with such a shallow wound." A somber expression moved across her features, sobering them as she gently touched his shoulder.

"It is often the shallow ones that bleed the most profusely." He murmured the words, trying to ignore the scents of fresh winter and warm cinnamon she carried with her.

And her curving body.

"For some reason, I am not as angry as I should be that you shot me."

"No?" She murmured the word, clearly distracted by her examination as gentle fingers moved over his skin.

Now that he was seated and she stood before him, each feminine sweep of her body was so close. Too close. Hips and breasts, revealed by the breeches and coat, were within reach of his suddenly needy hands. But Wulf did nothing except grip his knees, forcing his body to stay still.

"Have you previously injured your—" he paused to find the word "—prey?"

"No. A warning shot is usually all that is necessary, though I'm quite adept at wounding haystacks." Self-deprecation threaded through her words. "Surely, you are more practiced than I. You have been abroad. Seen war." Her hands paused as she reached for the buttons of his waistcoat. They hovered there, long fingers so still and steady they might have been carved from marble. "Fought for your beliefs."

"Yes." He might have said more, but her fingers began to briskly unbutton his waistcoat as if the pause in her movements had never happened.

"What was it like? Fighting, marching—doing something worthwhile?"

"Cold and hungry," Wulf said flatly. "But I wasn't a soldier for long. I was a spy."

———

"Well, that is news." Bea efficiently continued to unfasten the buttons, though her fingertips seemed to tingle now that she was so close to him.

Wulf's words were not a surprise. She had not suspected it before, but hearing him say it aloud seemed natural. She might have guessed the truth had her mind thought to consider the possibility.

The way his eyes saw right through a person, his sense of honor, the even temperament—and his easy acceptance of a highwayman as a makeshift surgeon. Wulf's adaptability would have proven useful as a spy.

"Such an appointment would suit you," she concluded. "I did not know you were assigned to espionage."

"I do not often speak of it. Few English drawing rooms are concerned with clandestine meetings in dank rooms in the French countryside. Not every cottage is as well-appointed as this one." He winced as she drew the waistcoat over his wounded arm. "But it is in the past. Unlike *your* secrets, mine are now of little interest."

"I suppose that is true." Bea dropped the waistcoat beside his other garments, studied the cravat he still wore. She wondered just what lay beneath that fine cloth and starched linen. Such broad shoulders filled the fabric, so able to bear the heavy burden of the dukedom. "Do you intend to expose me?"

Her hands were heavy as she lifted them to his cravat, but only because a strange anticipation filled them. She began to slowly unwind and loosen the starched fabric. With each movement, the space between them seemed to swell with something powerful, even mesmerizing. Bea looked into his lean, handsome face and caught the roguish gleam in his eyes.

She could not breathe.

"That remains to be seen." Wulf purred the words as the last loop of the cravat lifted away, revealing a squared jaw shadowed by stubble and the strong column of this throat.

Everything in her went warm and needy as he stared straight at her with heavy-lidded eyes. His gaze skipped hotly over her body, lingering here and there. The irises appeared black in the dim cabin, though she knew their color.

There was power in that gaze. Power and lust that sent licks of heat moving over her skin.

"I must maintain my reputation." Pulse quickening, she released the cravat and let it drop to the floor. "Such as it is."

She wanted to touch him. To skim her hand over that sharp jaw, feel the rasp of thick hair. Even lean down and set her lips to his.

"What may I call you, aside from the Honorable Highwayman?" The question rumbled from his chest, a low sound that skimmed over her senses. "You are undressing me, after all. Surely I might have your name?"

Four

She could not give him a name.

'Lady Beatrice Falk' would reveal everything, though Wulf would not likely remember the girl nine years his junior who dreamed of riding to the hunt and going to battle. He would not remember the woman careful to hide from her brother's drunken guests—for more than one reason.

But he would know the Falk name.

"That is a very long pause." Amusement twined through Wulf's deep voice. "I assume you are planning to lie?"

"I *did* intend to lie, but I cannot think of a proper one." It was the truth, which was no less dangerous than lies. "Nor will I give you my name—for obvious reasons."

"An honest highwayman, but not a foolhardy one." Callused fingers took her hand, brought it to his lips. Pressing a firm, sculpted mouth against her knuckles, he murmured, "In any case, it is a pleasure to meet you."

Her breath drew in. Pushed out. Flames crackled beside them, the howling wind fighting to penetrate the walls. Wulf kept her hand in his, watching her as if nothing else existed just then. It was an intoxicating sensation.

Bea drew back. His mouth was too full and sensual, his scent too strong. Everything about him made her want. And Bea knew the dangers of wanting and excess and lust. It did not matter if it was lust for drink, or pleasure, or dice, or silk.

Or making love.

Wulf would be a dangerous man to toy with. It would be too easy to fall under his spell and forget herself.

"Your wound still requires tending." Perhaps her body would cease this heady need if she focused on the practical. "If you would be so kind as to remove your shirt, it will be easier."

Bea did not wait for him to consent. She strode to the shelves lining the north wall and retrieved one of the iron kettles stacked there. Without bothering to don her greatcoat or scarf, she threw open the cottage door and stepped into the storm.

Wind whipped up a crystalline tempest to pelt her face. Ignoring the fury, she scooped snow into the pot. Icy cold stung her skin and made her fingers burn as she filled the kettle nearly to the brim. Then she wrestled the door closed and turned once more into the warmth.

Into Wulf.

He'd come up behind her, tall and half-naked as she'd commanded —and just *there*. His lips were close, and the thought of pressing her mouth to his filled her with need. She wanted to brush her fingers over the broad expanse of his chest and the blond hair sprinkled there.

"I thought it might be heavy." Wulf's voice was rough, his eyes dark with desire as he carefully removed the kettle from her hands.

He felt it as well, then, this tug between them.

"Perhaps it is the hit to my head that makes me take leave of my senses, but I believe this evening will be very—" he paused, pinning her with those deep blue eyes. "Engaging."

"Oh, do you?" Bea knew precisely what Wulf was thinking just then, and sent him a slow, knowing smile. "Clearly, you are not in your right mind."

"Oh, yes. I am in my right mind," he said softly.

His gaze was so hot, so dark, it set her body alight.

Dangerous, indeed.

"If you would bring the pot?" She moved around him, striding toward the fire and the chair. Giving herself to the Duke of Highrow would be foolish. She would risk too much, in too many ways.

Yet Wulf would make any woman cross the line.

Five

"I've no convenient petticoat to bind your arm with." Bea stared into the melting water. Little remained of the snow now, just a few swirls of white. Testing the surface with a fingertip, she judged it warm, but not hot.

She had begun to breathe properly again as she tended the water. Still, her body was tight, her mood edgy. Bea did not *want* to be cautious, but pleasure must always be approached with attention.

"We might as well use my shirt as a bandage," Wulf suggested. "'Tis a loss in any case."

The sound of rending fabric rose into the air as she removed the iron pot. She swirled the kettle once to even the water temperature, then turned to see him tearing strips from the bottom edge of his lawn shirt. He ripped again, firelight burnishing the shifting muscles in his shoulders.

She was no stranger to the male body, but Wulf's body was *more*. Masculine and virile and strong. And so very tempting.

Caution, she reminded herself.

Settling once more into the crude chair, he laid the strips of his ruined shirt over his thigh. White against the deep black. She strode forward, trying not to slosh the warmed water—but thinking of where that trail of blond hair led.

The one that disappeared beneath the waist of his breeches.

———

HER CINNAMON SCENT filled the air around Wulf again as his highwayman drew close. She set the water on the floor, then quickly unbuttoned her coat and shrugged out of it. Clad in shirtsleeves and a plain waistcoat, she leaned forward to study his wound.

The pain had dulled now—shoulder, head—giving way to an intense craving for her. One that balanced on the keen edge of pleasure and torment.

Competent fingers brushed against his thigh as she retrieved one of the cloth strips he'd laid there. Wulf went hard, fought not to touch her. To accept the gentle ministrations as she dipped the fabric in the water and carefully sponged away the blood.

She narrowed her eyes as she worked, leaned closer. He carefully studied each feature of her face, memorizing its contours. A strong nose, eyes he could see now were hazel, and a narrow, pointed chin. A lush, full mouth.

The dandies in London might not call her a diamond of the first water, but there was something arresting about her face, her confident manner.

"You are very beautiful," he murmured.

She stilled, frozen as she bent to reach for the pot of water again.

"No one has ever called me that before." Moving slowly, she dunked the cloth, then looked directly at him as she straightened. That level, honest stare was almost difficult to meet. "Someone said I was a handsome woman once, but no one has ever used the word beautiful."

"You *are* beautiful. It is true." So true, just the look of her dried his throat. Her face was fiercely lovely, full of feminine strength. Everything about those features might have come from an ancient goddess.

"Well. You are the first to think so." She breathed deep, let it out again, and continued her task. "If you intend to flatter me into becoming your lover, it will not work."

"I see." Amused at both of them, he studied her fingers as she worked. Long, quick, elegant. "Thank you for being straightforward about that."

"I am a highwayman, and I take my pleasure where and how I want, but I am careful." She slid him a mischievous glance, long lashes flashing over eyes not quite green, not quite brown, but a mixture of both. "And you are wounded."

"Hardly," he snorted.

"I must admit, I did a poor job shooting you." She probed the area gently, pursed her lips. "It is not even worth stitching, truth be told. Salve over the next few days and clean wrappings should do it."

"To be felled so low over so small a wound," Wulf quipped, and had the pleasure of seeing her lips turn up with humor.

"But felled by the Honest Highwayman, so that must be some comfort," she added.

"True." Which made him curious about her. She was certainly no village housewife or servant. "Who are you? It is whispered you give away everything you take. Why do you do this at all?"

"I am tempted not to tell you, but it is no secret among the villagers —though they may not answer if a duke were to ask." The used cloth plopped into the water as she abandoned it before reaching for the remaining strip of his shirt. "There are many in need. The lords write their laws, the orators in London shout about poverty and politics and money, but that does not change what is here. Right here, in the village. Many are prosperous, and many others are not. Children die of hunger from time to time, or the aged cannot pay for a surgeon or buy a tincture from an apothecary, and we lose them too soon."

"Few of my tenants are in such dire circumstances. I see that they are cared for during the lean times." Wulf disliked feeling the need to defend himself but found he could not let the statement remain unsaid.

"You are particularly kind, then." She wound the torn cloth around his shoulder, binding it tightly. "Many are not, and those in the village are unsupported. There was a young widow who gave away her four children a few years ago—to work for others for free, rather than as paid servants—because she could not feed them. They are fed and clothed now, so I cannot blame her. Yet I would have helped if I could. There are many who sit in London, in their finery and with their fancy brandy, visiting Parliament each day where they have a chance to make a difference." She breathed deep, then continued. "They think nothing of those who are less fortunate."

"I see." Perhaps Wulf might have been included among such company. He championed his own causes, but he had not often considered the circumstances of the poor. He doubted he would ever neglect the subject again. "Still, there are other, legitimate methods to see the poor are cared for. Pamphlets, treatises, even laws. Look to those who have made a difference before, making people think with their words. Skulking around at night and engaging in highway robbery is not necessarily the best method to support your cause."

"My method is practical, at least, and immediate." Annoyance flashed over her face. "Those I steal from possess more than enough money, and usually spend it on drink or gambling or women. Jewelry and fashionable gowns. New curtains for a drawing room, simply for the sake of new curtains." She tied the ends of the fabric and stepped back, examined her work.

"You rob those with excess and give to those in need." Fascinated, Wulf cocked his head, considered her firm expression. "And when you shoot your prey, you tend to his injuries."

"I suppose I do." Her lips slowly curved with resigned humor, softening the features that had hardened and making him want to kiss her as much as her irritation had.

He was certain there was not another woman in all of England quite like this one.

"You are an extraordinary woman."

She laughed at that. Threw back her head and laughed, long and loud. "You would not think so if we were anywhere but here, in this cabin."

"I think I would." Which brought another question to his mind. "Would I meet you somewhere else?"

"No." Though her smile remained and her gaze was steady, the word was flat. He had heard similar tones in the secret hiding places of France and Belgium.

"Why do I think you are lying?" he asked softly.

"Because I am a thief."

"True."

"I am also a passable surgeon." She grinned at him, eyes snapping once more with good humor. Stepping close, this time between his legs, she adjusted the binding on his arm with gentle hands. "You are quite cleaned up."

"Thank you, though it seems strange to say, as it was you who shot me."

Though she had no need to remain in front of him, she stayed, her thighs brushing against his. No petticoats and skirts between his skin and hers, only buckskin and wool. Wide, beautiful eyes met his, held. Still, she did not move away.

Heat speared through him, lust ground at his control. Her body called him. The nip at the waist of her waistcoat, the flare at her hips, the soft rounding of her belly. So many gorgeous lines and curves to follow. Unable to keep himself from touching, Wulf reached out with his good hand, set his fingers lightly on her waist.

Her breathing quickened, and her eyes went dark.

"Now that your injury is tended, what shall we do?" A feline smile moved across her face. "Games, perhaps?"

Six

Bea set her lips to his, took and tasted, simply because she wanted to. Caution be damned. The iron kettle on the floor was ignored, the shirt he'd discarded only a whisper in her mind.

Instead, the heat of him thrilled. The scent of him made her yearn.

And his mouth. It gave sweetly and still greedily consumed. He tasted of winter. Of lust. Of need. She wanted more before she even understood the want. Every inch of her body was lit with fire as brilliant and hot as the flame in the hearth.

Wulf's face tipped up toward hers. The hand at her waist curled around to her back, drew her closer as his injured arm rose. A warm, rough palm pressed against her cheek, his thumb feathering across her skin.

His strong thighs came together, holding her in place but not trapping her. Relishing the hard muscle against her softer curves, she let the sensation settle into her body, let it fuel her mouth. She moved her tongue over his lips, then pressed inside to tease.

Every movement simmered in her blood.

"Madam Highwayman," Wulf murmured. "Your mouth is more dangerous than your pistols."

In one strong, fluid move, he rose to his full height, the expanse of his chest filling her vision.

She *had* to touch.

His skin was smooth and hot. Muscle rippled beneath her fingers, the heat of his skin warming her cold fingertips. Though she felt the strain of his control, he waited. Daring, tempting, and releasing her all at once.

"Just how much do you want to play?" The rumble of his deep voice vibrated against her palm. "How far do you intend to go?"

"I don't know yet." But she knew how far she *wanted* to go.

"Decide." The tone of his voice lowered as he stepped closer, and she dropped her hand.

He was barely an inch away. She wanted to touch him again. More. Drawing her gaze upward, she let it linger on his mouth. Considered just what to do. Then two strong, callused palms cupped her face. Firm, hot lips bent to hers. Claimed.

His mouth sent lightning straight to her toes. Wrangled so much need and brought it to the surface. She could not stop her hands from roaming toward his shoulders, curving them around his neck, and settled her fingers in thick strands of blond hair.

Tugged a little. Just because.

His low, needy growl followed, and his mouth nipped once in response.

Suddenly she could not touch enough of him. Her hands roamed over his skin, down the muscled torso to grip his waist. The buttons of his fall-front breeches were just there, so she flicked them open. The breeches slipped to the floor to reveal—everything.

Long torso, strong thighs, and a body more than ready for her. She took him in her hand, reveled in the soft skin and hard strength.

"It is to my benefit you were only half-clothed," she murmured.

"And mine." Wulf's hands circled her waist, cupped her bottom and drew her close.

Bea abandoned her grip and pressed against him, the length of his arousal hard against her belly. She wanted him inside her, yet wanted this moment—this night—to last so much longer.

Wickedly, she grinned up into that lean, handsome face. "I have decided, Highrow. Making love is *exactly* what I will be doing tonight."

———

Approval roared through him.

He had wanted more of her than just a few kisses, a few touches. Had struggled against the fierce demand for more. He would have only gone as far as she would have allowed, but he was ridiculously satisfied by her choice.

He may not have survived otherwise.

Fueled by the haze of lust rushing through his blood, Wulf slanted his mouth over hers, continued to press that warm, feminine body against his. But it wasn't enough to drown in the scent of her, the taste of her mouth.

He had to touch.

Running his hands over rounded hips, over the soft waist, he aimed for the buttons on her waistcoat and quickly unfastened the tiny fabric-covered discs. She shrugged out of it herself while feathering kisses over his jaw. The nibbling touches pulled a growl from him and he began to untuck her shirt before her coat had even dropped to the floor.

White cotton followed dark wool a moment later, and she quickly removed the simple shift beneath her shirt, then her breeches—until she was standing naked before him. Gold and pink in the firelight, gaze fixed on his, and her full mouth lifted with wicked invitation.

The body hidden beneath the men's clothing was alluringly feminine. Heavy breasts, soft thighs. Dangerously curved and rounded. This was no slender willow, but a magnificent, lush woman.

Woman.

She might be the embodiment of the word.

Gorgeously confidant, she prowled across the room to one of the trunks. He had the pleasure of watching her round bottom as she retrieved a pile of blankets. She quickly spread one, then another, on the floor before the hearth. The remainder she laid aside, neatly piled for future use.

Neither of them were cold now.

"Come." Passion swirled in the word, seemed to rise from her skin as she held out a hand for him.

Wulf accepted, wanting his hands on every inch of her body. She drew him down to the blanket, then ranged herself over it. Stretching her arms over her head, she let him look his fill at a body he had not known he would crave so deeply.

He did crave her. Want her. *Need* her, as much as he needed his next breath. Everything he knew had tumbled away with the whirlwinds of snow, leaving only this passionate, powerfully sensual woman.

He could not quite regulate his breath, nor control the lust pounding through him. He slid his hands over her body, listened to her purr of approval. He took one breast in his mouth, tugged lightly at her nipple, and reveled in the tremble of her thighs even as she gripped his hair.

So responsive, so uninhibited. A man could lose himself in her passion.

He forgot everything beyond the circle of firelight, beyond the velvet of her skin, the heat that gripped him when he entered her. Her sigh of welcome shook his soul, her soft limbs drawing him in until he did not know where he was—except with *her*.

When his mind whirled like the storm outside and his blood burned like the fire indoors, he allowed himself to be lost in her.

Seven

The wood blazed once more as Wulf added fuel and stirred the coals back to life. Bea snuggled into the blankets he'd covered her with and let her gaze roam over his naked body. He was almost too exquisite to look at. Hard, lean, muscled. He had been a solder—a spy—and it showed still, even if he had been home for a few years. Certainly, he did not appear to be a duke.

But then, he was not supposed to be, until fate had played its hand.

"Do you miss your brother?" Bea wished she had not spoken the words as soon as they tumbled from her lips. The question was unpardonably rude, the answer entirely too private.

But he was staring at her over his shoulder, beautifully naked and carefully tending the fire. Everything about him had stilled, and she wondered if he had forgotten his important bits were not far from the flames.

"You know of my brother?" He set the poker aside and drew away from the hearth. Crawling over the pile of blankets and Bea herself, he settled himself beneath the covers and drew her close, leaving her near the warmth and his back to the cold room.

She resisted his embrace for a moment, but it was too pleasant to ease against his frame. To accept the heat of his body, the way his chest fit against her back. Watching the flames, aware of Wulf just behind her and doing the same, she said carefully, "I know you are not the firstborn."

Crackling flames filled the silence.

"I am sorry, Highrow. I should not have asked." Guilt rippled through her satiated body. "Please forget I did so."

"No. It is a good question, and I do not shy away from the truth." He dropped a kiss onto her bared shoulder, as if he had done such a thing a thousand times before. "I miss my brother very much, though not due to anything related to the dukedom. I simply miss my brother."

Everything in her sighed with sympathy. Poor Wulf.

"You were close."

"Very, but I rarely took the opportunity to return home once I became a spy. I had found a purpose in serving my country and pursued it relentlessly." The arm around her waist tightened, drawing her closer still to his hard, heated body. "He was gone just a few years later. I received word it was a fever of some kind."

"And so, you became the duke." Bea stared into the flames, trying to imagine such a moment. She loved her brother, though she did not always like him. Still, if he were gone, she would be mired in grief.

"And so, I became the duke." There was no bitterness in his voice. Instead, a deep sorrow coated his words. "My brother loved the land, the family. The title was at risk, and the history that went with it. I came home—to honor him. The family."

"You gave up espionage," she murmured.

"Family is more important." The hand circling around her waist drifted up to cup her breast. Easily, once again as if he had done so a thousand times before. But it was both the first time and the last, so Bea let herself enjoy the sensation of his callused hands on her skin. "Now Napoleon's missives have been exchanged for the grain yield."

"Do you miss it?" she asked.

"I miss my brother more." His fingers toyed with her nipple, each touch sending sparks through her. "Nor does it matter any longer. That life is gone. Forgotten."

"Nothing is ever forgotten. It is only behind you." Shifting within the circle of his arms, Bea turned to face him. Stared hard into those deep blue eyes. "Sometimes, you need to look behind you to determine where you are going."

"A philosophical highwayman." In the shadowed half-light, his face might have been carved from stone. Rough and strong, and blessed by the pagan gods.

"I am a highwayman of many parts." She pressed her lips to his. Softly, because she felt the hurt that still reverberated through his body. "You did what was right, coming home. You will continue to do what is right as the Duke of Highrow. Your brother would be proud."

"I hope so." He nibbled at the corner of her mouth, sending little shivers right down to her toes. "The wind has died down."

She had forgotten the snowstorm and the world beyond the warm cottage. It seemed as if, for a brief time, nothing existed outside the circle of golden firelight. Only the two of them, warm and naked and cocooned in blankets.

But morning would come, and with it a return to Lady Beatrice Falk, a spinster in her twenty-seventh year, and the commanding Duke of Highrow.

There would not be another man like him in her life.

No lover before, no lover after, could compare to Wulf.

"Dawn is only a few hours away," she whispered, cupping his cheek so the rough stubble brushed against the palm of her hand. "Will you make love to me again? Once more before the night is over?"

He did not answer her. Instead, he dipped his mouth to hers. Hot and firm and skilled, he seized the control she'd had only a while earlier. Heat swirled in her belly, clogged her lungs, as she ran her hands over his chest.

Mouth never leaving hers, Wulf continued to play with her tongue —teasing, tasting—as one hand drifted below to caress her hip, her bottom.

But his gaze had shuttered. He was different now, as though he'd reined himself in. From her body, from their conversations. She understood that. Knew he had lost himself the first time—and knew as if it had been she, just how terrifying that was. Control was as necessary as breathing or eating.

Could she give it to him? She did not know if she wanted to.

When he trailed his mouth between her breasts, she sighed. Let the licks and nips and kisses stir her desire. Sliding her hands upwards, she gripped the edge of the blanket and bared herself to him. He settled between her thighs, created magic with his fingers and mouth.

She wanted to stop him, to make him bend to her will instead of being lost in the need pulsing between them. In his caresses. In the pounding of her heart and the singing of her skin. Instead, Bea let his mouth and hands draw her up, bring her to pleasure, and lay her down again.

She opened her arms as she had before, wanting to bring him close to her again. Wulf shifted above her, arms braced on either side. His eyes, so deeply blue they held her captive, stared into hers.

"Who are you?" he whispered. "I want more of you. I don't want tomorrow to be the end."

"No one." A part of her soul broke away, the pain of it slicing through her. There was nothing for them, whatever she might want. "There is only tonight, Wulf. That is all."

His body was poised just at the entrance of hers. Hot, heavy. He held himself still, waiting. Thinking. Oh yes, he was thinking. And wanting.

"It is not enough." He pressed his lips to hers and thrust into her, the muscles in his arms and shoulders shifting beneath his skin.

"Only tonight," she repeated. Clamping her legs around his waist, she swung them around until she straddled him. Took him into her and rode him. "There is only tonight. We will make every moment count."

Eight

The thick blankets still enveloped him, but Wulf was alone in that warm soft wool. Morning light crept through the cottage windows, infusing the room with a white glow. The fire had died to embers, and the air had cooled enough he could see his breath.

Through the curling vapor, he saw her clothing was missing. The boots she'd set by the fire had disappeared.

The highwayman was gone. Without a goodbye, without a word.

Damnation! At the very least, she could have woken him. Instead, she'd stolen away in the dark.

Wulf shucked off the coverlet and rose into the chilled air to dress. Cursing again as the cold fabric touched his skin, he pulled on his breeches, then what was left of his tattered shirt. They had agreed to nothing, but the woman could have afforded him common courtesy at least and said goodbye.

Intent on leaving the cottage prepared for some other stranded traveler—or highwayman—he folded the blankets and replaced them in the trunk. She had already stacked the kettle on the shelf with its mates, so there was little to tidy. He spread the embers in the hearth and strode toward the door.

Setting his hand on the latch, he turned for one final look at the room. The simple table and chairs. The wide hearth. He would always remember her lying naked on the blankets, beautifully curved, her nipples a dusky pink.

That vision would be forever seared into his mind.

Part of him understood they should mean nothing to each other beyond shared passion. She was clearly a woman who went her own way. A highwayman, while he was a duke. They would not meet again, and that was for the best.

Bugger that. He wanted more than one night. Wanted more from her.

He opened the door to the cottage, the chill of the morning bolstering his sudden fury instead of cooling it. He would find her— find her, explain that one night was not enough, and make love to her again. Then once more.

Because she had made him think, made him feel. Made him want more deeply than he'd ever wanted.

She was *his* highwayman. For good or ill, and for how long, he did not know—but at least for a little while, they would belong to each other.

Assuming he could find her.

Pulling the door shut with a *snap*, he studied the clearing in front of the cottage. White blanketed everything, bringing with it a still winter silence. Small boot prints disturbed the smooth surface of the snow, pointing toward the shed. A little farther beyond, horse tracks arrowed toward the north. Toward the forest path, as far as he knew.

Wulf followed the tracks, each step in the ankle-deep snow increasing his discontent as the outside world crept back in. His stallion had disappeared, his shoulder was aching again, and his cursed high- wayman had left him stranded. He did not know precisely how far he was from his own estate, nor where the nearest tenant or villager's cottage might be.

Looking down at the horse tracks, he continued to follow them.

At least he knew where *she* was, and when he found her, he would wring the neck of that discourteous, beautiful, irritating, clever, sensual—

A wagon appeared on the path, bringing with it creaking wood and the muffled sound of hooves. A sway-backed mule led the weather-worn wood vehicle, its driver wizened and hunched against the cold—all three of them might be a century old.

"Yer Grace!" The driver reined in the mule, raised a hand, and wheezed, "I'm 'ere to get ye!"

"Is that so?" Wulf eyed the piles of fresh hay in the wagon bed, then the wrinkled face, red with cold. Surely the man was one foot in the grave and did not deserve to be out on a morning like this.

"The 'onest 'ighwayman sent me, Yer Grace. I'm to take ye home on me way to find work."

"I see. Thank you, then, sir." At least the blasted woman hadn't abandoned him entirely, though her gesture did not even his temper. "I would prefer to return to Falk Manor. Would you be so kind as to see me there?"

"'Spose." A frowned creased the old man's face. "I was going t'other way to pick up some work, but the 'ighwayman said as 'ow I ought to git you, and the jobs aren't plentiful anyhow. So, work can wait." He jerked his head toward the back of the wagon. "I've put out fresh hay."

"That is kind of you." Favoring his aching shoulder, Wulf pulled himself into the wagon and braced for the jolting ride. Even as he did so, he noted patches on the jacket draped over the hunched, frail shoulders in driver's seat. Surely the threadbare garment would not be warm enough for this bitter cold.

Yet the man was looking for work, despite shoulders bent with age.

Wulf thought of the Honest Highwayman's words the night before, of the poor and the old and infirm she provided for. Was this man one of Wulf's own tenants? He did not know, and could not say he would have paid attention before. He would not have looked. Really looked.

That shamed him, though he doubted he would ever fail to notice those around him again.

"My good sir," Wulf said, turning in the wagon and leaning against the planked wall. "Might I ask how long you have been acquainted with the Honest Highwayman?"

"Fer some time." The driver clucked to the mule and did not turn around. "I came to git yer, because I was asked. I won't say no more, for the 'ighwayman 'as done well by me."

Wulf had thought as much. The ancient man was one of the recipients of her thievery, and from the look of his frail frame, he could use it. "You are looking for work, you said?"

"Aye." The word carried a cautious tone. "Cutting ice, dragging it to the ice houses. The big families will want it come summer."

"Hm. Well, I've a need for another man in my stables, if he's good with animals and vehicles. Light repair to wheels and such, a bit of polish to the carriage lamps, currying the horses." Wulf rubbed at his chin, as if he wasn't thinking about that frail body hauling huge blocks of ice through the winter cold. "If you've the interest."

"Could be." The man clucked to the mule again, the sound inattentive rather than meaningful. "In the stables, you say?"

"Yes." He waited as the man glanced over his shoulder, consideration moving over weathered features. "Just present yourself at the rear door of Highrow Place if you've a mind."

The sound the aged driver made as they passed beneath the gate to Falk Manor was part grunt, part assent. Wulf accepted that as noncommittal, but noted he needed to speak with the head groom about finding a place for another set of hands should the offer be accepted.

The wagon trundled to a stop in front of Falk Manor's double doors, and the butler quickly opened them. Eyes wide, he examined the rough vehicle and the less-than-respectable appearance of both its occupants.

"Your Grace!" The butler called out as Wulf jumped from the wagon to stride up the front steps. "Has there been an accident? Are you injured?"

"I was delayed by a highwayman last evening and my horse bolted." He knew he sounded irritated and gruff, and smoothed his tone. "If I might seek assistance?"

"Of course, Your Grace." The butler glanced behind him as the lord of Falk Manor staggered across the parquet floor of the entryway, muttering something unintelligible. "His lordship," the butler murmured, "would be willing to offer whatever assistance you require."

"Thank you." Wulf eyed his host of the evening before.

The man still reeled from the effects of brandy and smelled like a perfumery. He appeared to have been sleeping, as his gaze was heavy-lidded and vague, and there were crease lines across his cheek.

"Highrow." The earl squinted one eye and focused on Wulf. "Are you back? If so, 'tis too late. My damned sister has rousted the lot of us, and the enjoyment is over. Everyone is off to bed."

"I am sorry to hear that." Not, of course, that he was. The fewer guests Wulf had to address, the better. Still, he decided to avoid mention of the Honest Highwayman altogether to the earl. "I was forced to shelter in the woods overnight. I thought perhaps I might impose upon you to arrange conveyance to Highrow Place."

"'Course." The earl turned to the butler, waved vaguely in the air. "Stewart?"

"I will send word to the stables to arrange a carriage." Stewart bowed to Wulf and spared his lordship not a glance—the butler was clearly accustomed to taking the reins of responsibility from his employer. "In the interim, I shall procure a room for you, where you might refresh yourself and perhaps break your fast."

"That would be most appreciated." Wulf ignored the earl as much as the butler had, which was just as well. His still-drunk host was listing sideways as he peered into the empty snifter in his hand.

"Your Grace," Stewart gestured toward the stairs leading to the upper floors. "If you would follow me—"

"*Bloody hell!*" Filled with utter fury, the feminine shout rang under the high, painted ceiling of the entryway and echoed long enough that the subsequent silence became ominous.

To a man, the occupants of the hall hunched their shoulders against that most terrifying thing—a woman's anger—and turned toward the sound.

Nine

The lady strode briskly through the sliding doors of the front drawing room, heels issuing a staccato beat on the polished parquet. Green flowers dotted her muslin gown, shifting over her skirts as if they marched along with as her temper.

"Did my brother ruin the drawing room rug? Truly? Mother took great care in bringing that from India ages ago. She would be heartbroken. There are burns. *Burns!*" The lady opened her arms wide, not in supplication or explanation, but as if to encompass the enormity of the transgression. A dusty paste bird nested in wigged curls just as the creature might have done during the woman's come out a decade earlier. "The rug is not meant for the ends of cheroots. Or brandy. There is an extensive spill—*Oh.*"

She stopped, blinked at Wulf through round, wire-rimmed spectacles. Her skirts floated to rest around her slippers, the embroidered flowers ending their patrol.

"My lady." He nodded in greeting, wincing because he should have addressed her as 'Lady Christian Name', but he could not remember her Christian name. He gestured to his wrinkled greatcoat, his bared head. "My apologies as to my appearance."

"Of course." A quick nod of her head, a flush of cheeks. "Your Grace."

He did remember the girl—woman now—from his childhood. He had seen her a handful of times since then, hovering at the fringes of her brother's house parties. Awkward in conversation but sweet in nature.

Desperately ready to wash, eat—and dear Lord, to sleep on a bed—Wulf turned back toward the butler. Stopped.

Cinnamon and woodsmoke.

He looked back, certain he was wrong. Sunlight reached beyond the lady's lenses, shining on eyes not quite green, not quite brown. Eyes he had not expected to see again. Not here, not so soon.

It was she.

His lover. His highwayman.

Everything in his body heated, hardened, flamed. He did not need to search her face for the truth. Did not need to think about it.

He simply *knew*. He'd learned each burst of green amid the warm brown of her eyes the night before, how the firelight played on them. They were different now in the bright sunlight and behind wire rims, but no less beautiful. More so.

His gaze dropped to her mouth, traced the full shape. Oh, yes, he knew those curves. Quite well. Other curves were hidden by the muslin gown, which sagged rather than clung, but he knew the contours of her lips.

The Honest Highwayman had been hiding in plain sight—behind ugly spectacles and elaborate, unfashionable wigs—but in plain sight, nonetheless.

"If you would be so kind, my lady, I should like to speak with you in the drawing room." He paused, pinned her with his gaze. "About the circumstances surrounding last night, of course."

He had found her now.

She would not escape again.

———

"There is no need." Bea coughed, sputtered.

"I insist, my lady." Wulf's dangerous tone shivered through her veins, though she tried to quell the rising panic that accompanied it.

Surely, he did not recognize her. No one ever suspected an aging spinster could *possibly* be the Honest Highwayman. Yet his eyes held cool steel—not the warm blue of the passionate lover she'd left sleeping at dawn.

"I don't—"

"Unless, of course, you would prefer to discuss various nighttime activities here in the hall?" His voice rumbled lower, warning Bea just how precarious her position was.

She looked toward her brother, already lurching up the steps to his bedchamber, then toward the butler who watched with guarded eyes. She could not see there was a choice.

"Very well, then." Wulf knew her secret—but she'd be damned if he held the reins for this particular reunion. Coolly, angling her head, she murmured, "Please join me in the drawing room, Your Grace."

Turning on her heel, Bea led him toward the chamber. She could feel his knowledge of her identity—her body—boring into her spine. If a few weeks had passed before they met again, he would not have identified her, and all would have been well. The night would have been nothing but a memory.

Damn him for arriving at Falk Manor instead of returning home.

Damn, damn, damn.

Bea was unprepared to meet him so soon in her spinster garb, had barely been able to set the night from her mind to attend to her other responsibilities. Just the sight of that wicked face and broad shoulders— knowing what was under the greatcoat—had her pulse scrambling.

The drawing room doors snapped shut before she was more than a few feet into the room. Bea swung around, prepared to argue, to defend, to lie.

And was swept up. By his scent, by his arms, by his mouth. Hungry and hot, his lips slanted over hers. Bea met his mouth with the same hunger because the want had been hiding beneath the surface of her skin. Waiting to surge through her blood and pound into her soul. Gripping his shoulders, she leaned into the kiss, into him, and reveled in the hard body pressed against hers.

Without releasing her, he drew back and looked at her. Just looked. Beyond the spectacles, beyond the blasted wig.

"You are an extraordinary woman." He'd said the same words before, in those moments trapped between snowstorm and firelight. "Hello, my Honorable Highwayman."

"I suppose the jig is up." It stung her pride to be discovered, yet there was relief in sharing the secret. Even for a few moments. "Will you turn me over to the magistrate?"

"I'm considering it." His mouth came back to hers, tasted and took and gave in the most delicious way. "If you ever leave my bed again without waking me to say goodbye, I most certainly will."

"I *beg* your pardon?" Bea drew back, looked hard into those dark blue eyes.

"You don't think for one minute that we are done, do you? I don't want last night to be the end." Gently, he reached for her spectacles, removed them. "Do you need these?"

"Not at all." There was no point in more lies, so she took the spectacles and slipped them into the pocket of her gown. "They are only glass."

"The wig?" He flicked a finger at the dull brown curl dangling over her left ear.

"Useful." Bea tugged at the wig, pulling at pins and scattering them about. She dropped the monstrosity of hair and paste and powder onto the ruined rug, then shook out her cropped natural locks. Reveled in the release of the weight, as she always did.

"*There* you are." He framed her face with his large hands, studied it. "You are more beautiful in the daylight than you were in the firelight."

"Oh, Wulf, that is nonsense." But it delighted her nonetheless.

"It is true. No, the London dandies would not cater to you, and perhaps you would not have your pick of the marriageable gentlemen—"

"Oh, well," she said dryly. "That's flattering."

"Wait." He laughed and slid his arms around to circle her waist. "You don't need the dandies and the gowns and jewels to be beautiful, which is what they judge beauty by."

"No?" She should not be turning into a puddle with such words, but she was.

"You are beautiful because of something else altogether." His mouth pressed against hers, soft and sweet. "Your heart."

Damn him again. Her knees went weak.

"Wulfric Standover, you are a rogue." At his bland expression, she added, "A sentimental one, but a rogue nonetheless. Which you know."

"I know nothing."

"That line belongs to the highwayman of our little scene."

"So it does." He traced her mouth with a finger, then the edge of her jaw. That finger slid down the neck to play with her collarbone. "Might I have the pleasure of your name now?"

"Beatrice." She paused, because it mattered that he used the name she had given to herself. "Bea."

"It is a pleasure to meet you again." As he had in the cottage, Wulf raised her hand to his lips. The calluses of his fingers were no less exciting, the touch of his mouth no less thrilling. "Bea."

Her body shuddered and yearned, just as it had then. Pressing herself against his wide chest, Bea raised her mouth for a kiss. His lips molded to hers, so ready to provide just what she wanted.

"The butler is likely wondering what is happening behind the closed doors," she murmured against his mouth. "My brother is gone to bed, of course, not that he would notice or care, particularly."

"I would say 'let them wonder,' but you have a reputation to maintain." He drew back, raised one blond, wicked brow. "Of sorts."

"If a spinster of twenty-seven cannot take a lover, then the world is a dreary place indeed." Bea pursed her lips. "Now that you know who I am, I'm quite inclined. It would be a novel experience to make love with a man who knows both the spinster and the highwayman."

"What if I choose not to settle for just a lover?" Even as he spoke the words, Wulf appeared as shocked as Bea felt. Then his shock smoothed away and determination replaced it. "What if I want more?"

More than lovers? What was there? Bea could only see marriage, and she was not at all certain she wanted to be under someone else's control in such a way.

"I may not have more to give, Wulf." In fact, she was certain of it.

"With a heart as deep as yours, I know you do." He swung her back into his arms. Strong, kind arms that did not restrain her. They only held her carefully, as if avoiding hurt or caging, before he claimed her lips for a deep kiss. "It is not a discussion for today, however. Today I only ask for a bath, breakfast, a decent bed—with you in it—and tomorrow we shall see what we see."

Tomorrow.

Tomorrow might be filled with lovemaking and laughter, if Wulf was there. With conversation that did not involve gambling and brandy. With something deeper, if she could be open to it.

She might be.

"Today we shall see to breakfast and beds and—" she grinned wickedly at him. "Loving."

"I am ready for that, as these moments in the proper drawing room are a torture. I am already seeing your gorgeous body on a soft bed, where I can love my highwayman properly." He drew her close, set his lips to the curve of her neck. "Tomorrow and the next day, then, and we shall see to the rest."

Bea could not fault that logic, so she settled into the circle of his arms and let Wulf kiss her senseless.

Epilogue

"Stand and deliver!"

The shout echoed between tree trunks and shivered leaves the deep green of mid-summer.

Wulf did not shift in the saddle nor change the pace of his gelding. He'd heard that voice before, exactly in this spot on the worn dirt path between oaks and firs and thick brush.

It was her favorite location for highway robbery.

"Damn you, Wulf, you were supposed to at least *pretend* I was still a highwayman." With that annoyed shout, the love of his life burst through the tree line just ahead of him at a full gallop. As Bea often did now, she wore her gold-brown curls loose. They streamed behind her, whipping in the wind and longer than they had been over a year before when they had met.

Perhaps a better phrase would be when he first met the Honorable Highwayman and fell in love with her.

As Bea's mare thundered to a stop beside him, Wulf reined in his horse and dismounted. She slipped from the saddle a moment later and he slid his hand beneath her hair. Cupping the nape of her neck to pull her close, he set his lips on hers. Warm and sweet, her mouth curved beneath his and set his blood humming.

She was the most precious thing in his life.

Bea.

"I did not expect you to return until tomorrow," she murmured, drawing back as the animals settled. Her hand slipped into his, their fingers linking together as they had a thousand times before.

"I could not wait," Wulf said simply. With Bea there was no need to guard his words, nor did she do so. At first, they had warily circled each other, each careful not to allow the other too close, but no longer. "There was no sense in staying in London when you were here."

Her wide, full lips moved with the same slow curve every time. As if her smile needed time to build, to grow from within, before it could be released to the world. "Then tell me your news."

"As always, it is business before pleasure for you." Wulf laughed they fell into step, leading their horses along the forest path between Falk Manor and the crossroads that would take him own estate. "The bill for widows and orphans is under consideration. Parliament is on recess and will reconvene in the fall. I do not know how many will read the bill before we return, but it will be up for debate and vote."

"That is something, at least." She nodded once, mouth firming. "If the issue of the poor is placed in front of them often enough, they will eventually see the truth."

Wulf was not entirely certain, knowing the perfidy of the House of Lords and House of Commons, but there was no other way to effect laws beyond going to Parliament.

"We worked together to draft the bill," he said. "We'll do so again next session if need be. Although, with the war going on, I am not certain anyone will pay attention."

"Then we will make them." Confidence rode on Bea's shoulders, squaring them beneath a proper riding habit he did not know she even owned before today. He usually saw her in ragged breeches on a horse or wearing pretty gowns during the day, and as often as he could, wearing nothing at all. Perhaps tonight—

"Maybe not in my lifetime, or yours," she continued, unaware of the direction his thoughts had taken. "But if we speak, others will hear."

They walked silently for a few moments, their soft footfalls on the path a counterpoint to the clop of the horse's hooves. Sunshine dappled the ground around them, shown on Bea's hair and sparked the gold hidden in the brown depths. Without the need to disguise herself any longer, she had let her hair grow free. It suited her, that slightly wild tangle of curls she rarely bothered to bind up. With her cheeks pink from her ride and the green velvet of her habit, she might have been a painting entitled *Summer*.

She was meant to be out of doors, not in the drawing room.

"Do you miss being a highwayman?" he asked softly. He focused his gaze on her profile, the strong nose, the pointed chin. One corner of her full lips turned up in an expression he had learned to recognize as both amused and wistful.

"Yes." She spoke as quietly as he, as though carefully weighing her words. "But there is little need for the Honest Highwayman now that you have gathered the local landowners and persuaded them to better care for their tenants. It is time to fight the battle elsewhere."

"Do you need a new challenge, then, Bea?" He raised their joined hands to his mouth and kissed her sun-warmed skin.

Now she snorted. "Living with my brother is challenging enough—though he has been brought around a bit to the idea of caring for the tenants and villagers. Still, he continues to host those ridiculous house parties. The guests all seem to enjoy themselves, but they are a trial for the servants, what with the constant refilling of glasses and the messes left behind. Wulf, I swear to you, I have scrubbed the rug in the drawing room a dozen times this past year."

She looked up at him, brows raised and voice full of exasperation. Then her smile bloomed again. "I am glad you are home, Wulf. I missed you terribly."

"Then marry me." The words popped out before he was ready to say them. And yet they had been swirling in his mind for months. He had not asked before because Bea was filled with such spirit, he feared she would feel constrained by marriage.

Or that she would refuse him.

But it was too late now.

"Marry me, Lady Beatrice Falk."

She had stopped walking, her face turned up toward his. Hazel eyes flickered over him, studying each feature as if to ascertain his veracity. Around them, birds called and fluttered in the trees while the wind whispered through their leaves.

"Why?" she finally asked.

"What?" Wulf couldn't decide if her words were a punch to his belly or if he simply hadn't heard her correctly.

"Why? Why do you want to marry me?" Oh, yes, she was quite serious. The set of her pointed chin was firm, her lips pressed tightly together.

"Because I love you. Why the hell else?" Frustrated, he dropped his horse's reins to run his hands through his hair, then quickly snatched them up again lest the animal bolt. "What do you think we have been doing this past year and more?"

"Enjoying each other's company." She spoke calmly, but her eyes were wide now. "You love me?"

"Oh, Bea," he breathed. Quickly, Wulf took the reins of both horses and tethered the animals to a nearby tree, allowing them to clip grass as they chose. When he turned back to Bea, he found her watching him, eyes wary, arms folded so the gold fastenings of the trim riding habit were hidden.

"I do love you, Bea. I'm not sure when it happened, but it was somewhere between having you lodge a bullet in my shoulder and then sneaking away before morning." It was true. He remembered every moment of that night in the cottage, and every moment since.

The wind picked up, ruffling her hair and snatching at her skirts. Mid-summer flowers lining the path danced in the breeze and birds swooped above them, reveling in the sunshine as they called to one another.

Still, she did not move.

His heart began to pound, a frantic beat that seemed to echo in his ears as he waited for her to speak. Perhaps she *would* refuse him. As an unmarried woman, she had complete control over her life. Becoming a duchess would change everything.

"Well," Bea finally said. "I supposed that is convenient, as I love you too."

And she threw herself into his arms in a flurry of windswept curls and green velvet.

THE END

Season of Scandal

One

"What will your father say when he finds out?" Lady Heatherstone wrung her hands as their carriage rolled to a stop, the feathers in her hair shivering along with her movements. "He'll most certainly have an apoplexy tomorrow morning when he discovers what you've done—and I shall die of mortification this evening!"

"I do not think it is scientifically possible to expire of mortification, Mother," Prue answered drily. As the carriage door opened and the steps were set down, she adjusted her half-mask, checking the ribbons to ensure it was in place. She did not particularly care if the other ball guests knew she was Miss Prudence Chapman, daughter of Baron Heatherstone—it was her Season of Scandal, after all—but one never knew what would happen at the annual masquerade.

This year promised to be the best yet, as the theme was Shakespeare's *A Midsummer Night's Dream.*

Perhaps Prue would meet a tall, dark stranger who would sweep her off her feet. Perhaps she would meet Oberon, the king of the fairies, who would fall instantly in love with her and take her back to his fairy kingdom as his queen.

Prue snorted at her own idiocy. In Shakespeare's play, there already *was* a queen of the fairies. Titania. Moreover, what man in his right mind would pursue a female guest costumed as a soldier, complete with breeches and Hessian boots?

And the only man who could sweep Prue off her feet had left for battle long ago.

The bastard.

Prue ignored the hand the footman offered and jumped out of the carriage to join her mother on the cobbled London street. If a lady had the freedom of wearing breeches and boots, she ought to take advantage of both.

"Mother, it will be fine." Prue squeezed her mother's hand in reassurance. "I have not had a marriage offer in all the time I've been on the Marriage Mart. There is nothing I can or cannot do that will change my prospects. I'm firmly on the shelf."

For six years she had done what the *ton* expected. She had toed the line, danced, smiled, sung—but as soon as she opened her mouth to say something intelligent, she was a lost cause.

"But your—your—*limbs*. They are visible." Lady Heatherstone's voice rose to a panicked squeak as they ascended the steps of Whitwell House. "It is indecent. Scandalous. Prue, you cannot possibly enter a Society ball dressed in such a way."

"Mother, at this point, I can do whatever I want. I have no prospects as it relates to a husband, and I do not want them. I have the settlement from Aunt Mary, so I needn't worry about money." She laughed lightly as they reached the door. "I am, quite simply, free."

For the first time in her life.

Even if her parents turned her out, even if the *ton* turned their collective backs on her, Prue could support herself and do as she chose. No one could tell her differently. Come what may.

Freedom was a delicious feeling—and decidedly exciting.

Though it was only May, the evening seemed to resonate with the magic of Midsummer's Eve. The longest day of the year—when anything could happen.

Perhaps she *would* find a handsome fairy prince this evening.

And do all the wicked things she wanted to.

———

He heard the murmurs long before he saw her.

Who is she?

Scandalous!

What do you suppose she means by it?

A soldier! How preposterous!

"What has the *ton* in a state now?" As far as Noah Clarke, the Earl of Parkwood, was concerned, the *ton* was always in a state. Noah pressed one forefinger at the slight ache making itself known between his brows. He wished he were anywhere but standing in Lord and Lady Whitwell's ballroom—yet here he was, wearing the ubiquitous half-mask and black cape over his evening wear.

"Oh, I say." Noah's companion, Lord Hawksbury, fumbled for his quizzing glass and held it up to his eye. Even costumed as a footman, Hawksbury had brought the accessory. Gazing through the lens, he nodded his head to a spot somewhere behind Noah's right shoulder. "I should think a woman dressed like *that* would cause a fuss."

Noah turned, expecting yet one more Greek goddess, an elaborately costumed fairy, or perhaps the dozenth Titania or Helena of the evening.

Instead, a soldier stood in the doorway to the ballroom, not ten feet away from him. After a single glance, he understood the murmurs of the guests. This soldier was unlike any Noah had seen during his many battles on the Continent.

The sight of her stole the air from his lungs, though he could not see her face beneath the white half-mask. But he could see gray breeches molded to rounded hips and thighs, and a trim, tight-fitting crimson coat hugging her torso. A soldier's shoulder belt crossed between a stunning bosom and ended with a holster at her hip. Below her mask, wide, full lips curved in an amused half-smile that simply begged to be kissed.

But there was something else about her entirely, more than her shape or the uniform, that tugged at Noah. She exuded an air of daring, of confidence, that the other ladies simply did not have.

This soldier, this woman, was prepared for whispers and rumors, and reveled in them.

Her hand slid over one hip in a tantalizing movement that ended with long, slim fingers resting on the holster of her shoulder belt.

Devil take it. She carried a pistol in the holster.

He hoped the weapon was not loaded. Or that she did not shoot her foot off.

"Do you recognize her?" Noah murmured to Hawksbury, his gaze focused on the butt of the weapon. "I've not been back in the *ton* long enough that she is familiar to me." He had been far too busy carving out his career as a captain—until Fate and the morbid sore throat changed the course of his life.

"I cannot say I know her," Hawksbury answered just as softly, still eyeing the woman through his quizzing glass. "She is neither tall, nor particularly short, and her hair is quite a non-descript shade of brown, so that is no help a'tall in identifying her."

Noah narrowed his eyes and studied the woman as she moved farther into the ballroom. She wore no bicorn or shako as part of her uniform, so her hair was loose and fell nearly to her waist. "I would not call her hair color non-descript," he said, deciding that the deep brown was not quite curly, not quite straight. If he could capture it in a single instant, he would describe the texture of her hair as wind rippling over a hayfield. "I would suggest her hair is an interesting shade of chocolate."

"Is that so?" Hawksbury turned the quizzing glass on Noah, brows raised in speculation.

"Get that glass out of your eye, Hawksbury. You look ridiculous, particularly with the half-mask." So the man did, the way the glass magnified his iris. Moreover, Noah knew perfectly well Hawksbury did not need it to see.

"Mayhap you should make the acquaintance of our little chocolate-haired friend, eh?" Hawksbury dropped the quizzing glass. It bumped against the waistcoat of the footman's livery he wore. "Given tonight's theme, anything might happen if you believe in fairies."

"So it might." Noah had not wanted to attend the masquerade. He had never wanted his brother's title. Yet suddenly he did not mind standing here in the Whitwell's ballroom.

As if the soldier unerringly knew her target, the woman turned her head and met Noah's gaze. It was as if he were struck by an arrow, one that pierced both mind and chest. He could not see the color of her eyes, nor even the shape of them, but he felt her gaze penetrate every fiber of his being and knew he wanted her to be his—at least for this evening.

Her smile widened, a tantalizing curve of pink, and he realized it was not amusement she exuded, but excitement. Even anticipation.

"Anything might happen," Noah repeated. As he threaded through the other guests, ignoring fluttering fans, overbright laughter, and a bevy of fairy wings, he held the soldier's gaze and tried to ignore the light smile flirting with the corners of her mouth.

"Either way," he murmured to the ballroom in general, "the evening is suddenly a great deal more entertaining."

Two

"Y ou are not quite what I expected for my prince this night." The soldier tossed her head and looked up at Noah, that rich, chocolate hair shifting over her shoulders in a riot of waves. "You did not choose to be Oberon, King of the Fairies? Nor even Theseus, the Duke of Athens? You are not following the theme of Shakespeare's play, sir."

"I cannot say you are either." He raised one brow. "A soldier? Quite a daring costume."

"We are celebrating the exile of Napoleon, are we not? It seemed appropriate." Beneath the edge of the white half-mask, her lips curved into a wide smile, revealing an alluring dimple. "Moreover, I suspected there would be dozens of Titanias and Helenas and fairies this evening. I would never wish to be so predictable."

"Somehow, I doubt you ever could be predictable." He wanted to see beneath her mask, though now that he was close, he noted her eyes were the same rich shade as her hair. Noah was aware of candles playing over sparkling gowns and what seemed acres of flowers in the ballroom, but he could only focus on her.

"You would be surprised at how predictable—and even tedious—I am. Still, I am not as uninteresting as your costume." Her gaze flicked over him, head to toe, even as she flicked a finger against the edge of his black cape. "Just *this* over your evening wear? Could you not find something better?"

"What would you consider interesting?" He pitched his voice low and was rewarded with a knowing smile.

"Well, there appears to be a Bottom over there—you know, the leader of the actors from the play?" She slid her gaze toward Noah, even as she tipped her head toward the other side of the crowded ballroom. "*That* is a much more interesting costume."

He followed her gesture, past a Greek goddess, a fairy in sparkling gold, three Titanias, and blinked—then barked out a laugh before he could stop himself. "Is that gentleman wearing a papier-mache donkey head?"

"So it appears. The ears are rather...large, do you not think?" Amusement threaded through her voice, and when Noah turned back to his soldier, he saw her dimple had winked into existence once more. "You know the fairies gave Bottom the head of an ass in the play, do you not?" she said.

"So I recall. 'O Bottom, thou are changed. What do I see on thee?'" he quoted.

"'What do you see?'" She laughed softly, a low and husky sound that brought to mind dark corners and tangled limbs rather than the costumed guests around them. "'You see an ass-head of your own, do you?'"

Noah raised his brows and leaned toward her. "You are familiar with the play, then."

"I am familiar with a great many things." The suggestive look she sent him hinted at both mystery and daring, and set his blood pounding. "What I know rarely appeals to anyone, least of all the *ton*."

"I find that surprising." He found *her* surprising. "You are by far the most fascinating woman here—not least of all because of your costume. What concerns me at present, however, is whether your weapon is loaded." Noah nodded toward the shoulder belt and holster at her hip. The butt of the pistol was heavily engraved silver and polished to a shine. Certainly not standard issue for the infantry, but a weapon commissioned from a master.

"Of course, the weapon is loaded." One dark brow rose above the edge of her demi-mask. "What use is an empty pistol?"

"Damnation." She *would* shoot her foot off, or another guest's foot. "Carrying a loaded pistol when you don't know how to use it is of the utmost stupidity."

"That is rather narrow-minded as it relates to the abilities of women, do you not think?" Something dangerous flickered in the depths of her eyes. Despite himself, Noah found he could not look away from her.

Was his statement narrow-minded? No woman he had ever known used a pistol, let alone properly—except one, a long time ago. And that woman was likely long married by now.

"I suppose my statement was both unfair and uninformed," he conceded, though he could not stop himself from challenging her. "Can you use the weapon, then?"

"Of course." She fisted one hand on her waist, cocked her hip, and leveled him with eyes full of challenge. "I can demonstrate, if you like."

"Perhaps not at the moment. It might send Lady Whitwell into a swoon if you set off a pistol in her ballroom." Speculatively, he ran his gaze over her. Intrigued by the set of her chin, he leaned closer. Her scent was light and clean, and rose above the candlewax and perfumes that pervaded the ballroom. Nothing cloying for Mistress Soldier. "How much do you know of weaponry?"

"I know quite a bit about pistols," she said huskily, tipping her face up toward his. "And swordplay."

Lust flooded him. The scent of her, the sound of her, every word pulsed into him. He fought to contain that hot flash. "'There is a double meaning in that.'"

"Wrong Shakespeare play, my dear sir." She laughed, eyes brightening behind the mask. "That quote is from *Much Ado About Nothing*."

Violin strains filtered through laughter and speech, and Noah glanced toward the musicians. Bows were laid over strings, nimble fingers turned tuning pegs—a new set of dances would soon be starting.

"Would you do me the honor of this set?" He offered her a short bow, feeling ridiculous in the cape, but determined to keep her with him. "Unless, of course, you have promised it to another."

"I have not, and should like nothing better than to dance with you."

Noah offered his hand and she placed hers in it. She wore no gloves, and when he brought her fingers to his lips, he lingered a moment over her soft skin. "I am most honored, Miss…"

"Oh, no." Her laugh was ripe with an edge of sensuality that teased the senses as Noah ushered her onto the smooth, parquet dance floor. "'Tis a masquerade. Is it not the point of a masquerade to hide one's identity?"

As Noah stepped into his place in line, his gaze never left hers. "Only until the unmasking at midnight."

———

She was tempting Fate.

Prue knew it, but every inch of her skin was alive.

Oh, but his eyes were brilliant behind the black mask. Cobalt blue and intense in both color and concentration, Prue held his strong gaze even as they took their places in line for the country dance.

This was the man she had been waiting for. The Season had started months ago, and though she had behaved as she'd wanted this year, Prue had yet to find a man to give her what she craved—stolen moments, drugging kisses. More, perhaps, if she were always to be spinster.

Because there was certainly more.

The music began and they clasped hands, the couple they were paired with doing the same to create a four-pointed star. Around they went, first one way, then changing hands and directions to move the opposite way. There was no opportunity for conversation with the other couple between them—but Prue heard the conversation with her caped partner just the same.

How much do you dare reveal? his deep blue eyes asked, his gaze never leaving hers.

Wearing a soldier's uniform as your costume, would you dare to be more scandalous?

Will you be scandalous with me?

They broke apart from the other couple and Prue set her hand on the stranger's arm—though he did not seem a stranger. She glanced up as they moved between the row of dancers, stepping in time with the music. Already the strong profile of his nose seemed familiar, and she knew the shape of his lips. The top lip was thin, perhaps, but his bottom lip was full and ripe and promised something wicked and wonderful.

"If we are not to reveal our identities, what should I call you, then?" He bent slightly to murmur the words into her ear. "Mistress Soldier seems unfit."

"You shall have to think of something, I suppose." Prue laughed lightly as they turned to promenade back to their places. "I shall have to think of something as well. Unless—do you have a title, perhaps? Duke or viscount? Baron?"

"Ah, but if I reveal my title, then you may discover who I am."

"So you *do* have a title." Raising her brows, Prue took her place once more in the row. They clasped hands and stepped forward to meet in the center while the strains of violins swirled through the ballroom. Though there were inches between them, she swore she could feel the heat of his body. They stepped back again, then forward once more. He spun her, just as every other man had done during every country dance since her come out—yet everything inside her went liquid and hot with this man. "Perhaps we have met before, then?"

Damn it all, she was breathless even without her stays.

"Perhaps. Perhaps not." His lips curved up in a roguish grin. "I daresay I would remember a lady in breeches."

They separated, took new partners to move about in a circle—yet Prue paid little attention to her new partner, performing the steps by rote. Her focus was entirely on the stranger in the black cape with the cobalt eyes.

"It is singularly freeing to dance in breeches," she said as she took her partner's hand once more. "I am not certain I shall ever revert to stays again."

"But then I should miss out on the view of your lovely bosom in a gown."

His words were outrageous. Dangerous. *Delicious.*

Full of all the daring she had stifled for six long years, the reckless-ness she had never been bold enough to reveal, Prue shook back her hair and looked up into his face. "Who dictates that a bosom can only be viewed in a gown?"

Oh, by all the Fates, did those words come from her?

They had, and though they were once again promenading between other couples, Prue knew nothing but the swirl of the stranger's cloak, the sharp line of his jaw, the overly long hair brushing against his collar.

He leaned over, as if imparting some innocuous comment, and pressed his lips just closer to her ear than was proper. "Shall we take a turn about the terrace, my warrior?"

"Warrior? Is that what you have decided to call me?" The country dance was not even over, yet she accepted his gloved hand in acquiescence and left her place in line to lead him away from the dance floor.

It was, perhaps, the most outrageous thing she had done to date, abandoning the dancing in full view of the *ton*. Oh, she saw the sidelong glances of the prudish mamas, the shock of the debutantes.

She did not care one whit. When a woman was on the shelf and ready for the scandal of her life, a few frowns did not matter.

Prue looked up into the masked face of her partner. "I suppose the terrace is a better location to experience scandal than the ballroom."

Three

"Scandal?" Noah repeated. The sounds of the ballroom faded slightly as they stepped onto the long, flagstone terrace, though light still gleamed through the windows and the violins sounded faintly on the night air.

"I am quite firmly on the shelf, sir." The woman turned to face him and leaned against the balustrade of the terrace. Did she have any idea how attractive her legs were in breeches? It was no wonder mothers insisted their daughters wear skirts. "I am also independently wealthy. I need no husband, and do not intend to have one. I am only here to appease my mother for one final season before I set up my own household, Society be damned. Therefore, I have chosen to do as I please this Season. That includes engaging in however many scandals I choose."

"Including wearing a soldier's uniform to a ball?" Noah gestured to her costume.

"And other things." The husky tone of her voice fed the stirring in his blood. "Including spending time with a strange man on a dark terrace."

"I am surprised you are on the shelf." Not with those full, pink lips and the breasts showcased by the shoulder belt. "Certainly some gentleman of the *ton* would have offered for you."

"Ah, but I am quite plain beneath this mask, and considered a blue-stocking, if truth be told." She cocked her head to one side, the light from inside Whitwell House gleaming over her. With the dark garden beyond her, she seemed to glow. "Why did you call me warrior? 'Tis an interesting choice."

"Infantryman seemed too simple." Noah moved beside her and leaned his elbows on the balustrade so that they stood side by side, she facing Whitwell House, he the gardens, resplendent with spring flowers, winding paths, and thick hedges.

"Dragoon?" he continued. "Life Guard? Foot Guard? There are the Rifles, of course, the Highlanders, Engineers, Artillerymen, Quarter-masters, Cavalry—but none of those would do, would they?" Noah tried not to let the bitterness of his military career escape, but he was certain he failed. "You are someone entirely different, fighting an entirely different war in the ballrooms of London."

"'We cannot fight for love, as men may do.'" She spoke softly, never leaving her position on the balustrade, though she turned her head to look at him. Light slanted over her face, and for a moment he thought he could see beyond the half-mask to the features behind it. Then the impression faded, and she became a stranger once more.

"If I recall from the play, the fair Helena spoke those words," he said.

"Indeed. You are familiar with the play as well, then?"

"My tutors forced me to read every Shakespeare work over and over until I could pluck quotes from thin air." During the dark nights of a campaign on the Continent, he had found rereading the plays in the privacy of his officer's tent allowed him to avoid the painful memories of what he had left behind.

"A useful talent at times, no doubt." She shifted slightly, her arm brushing against his as she smiled cheekily at him. "Do you use it to charm ladies?"

"'Shall I compare thee to a summer's day? Thou art more lovely and more temperate. Rough winds do shake the darling buds of May—'"

"Oh, do not resort to such common quotes!" Her laughter was full-throated and delighted. "That is a sonnet everyone has read and memo-rized, no doubt. Such words do not sway me."

"Very well, then, I shall think of something better." Noah straightened and reached for her hand. He drew her along the terrace, away from lighted windows and into the shadows. "As I was not able to impress you with my costume as much as a man with a papier-mache donkey head, I shall have to try harder."

"You must admit, it is a difficult impression to best. His painted smile really was quite well done." She laughed again, more lightly this time.

They paused at the end of the terrace, just at the steps leading to the gardens.

"You have a beautiful laugh," he murmured. He could not see her eyes in the darkness, but he heard her breath catch and saw her lips part slightly. Moonlight washed over her face, silvering the skin of her cheeks and the curve of her mouth.

Unable to stop the need to touch her, he removed his gloves, slowly, finger by finger, as she watched him steadily. Waiting. Anticipation built between them, as palpable and solid as if he could see it. He dropped the gloves to the terrace floor, intent only on her, and gently set his forefinger on her mouth.

Slowly, lingeringly, he drew his finger across her lips.

"'I pray thee, gentle mortal, sing again:
Mine ear is much enamour'd of thy note;
So is mine eye enthralled to thy shape;
And thy fair virtue's force perforce doth move me
On the first view to say, to swear, I love thee.'"

Her breath shuddered out, and for a moment she did not move. They might have been frozen in the moonlight, two marble statues. Then her tongue touched his finger, softly, tantalizingly.

"At least you quoted from *A Midsummer Night's Dream* this time," she whispered.

Noah stared down at her, unable to read her expression, but he knew the need that thundered in his veins, heard her deep inhale and felt the subtle tremble of her body. Cupping her cheeks, he bent his head until their mouths were but a whisper apart.

He craved even just the briefest kiss, the lightest touch. He did not know if she felt the same yearning, but Noah knew he could no more stop himself from kissing her than he had been able to keep from touching her.

Still, he hesitated, trying to read those deep, chocolate eyes hidden by the night and breathing in the scent of her light perfume, the leather of the shoulder belt, the air fragrant with spring flowers.

Waiting, he could only revel in the softness of her skin.

Wanting, he could only hear the beat of his own blood.

———

IF PRUE HAD WANTED SCANDAL, she had found it.

In *him*.

His words were only a quote, nothing more than that. Yet she felt each syllable resonate in her body. She moved forward, her body brushing ever so slightly against his. Beneath the wool of the uniform coat, beneath the linen shirt, her breasts suddenly began to feel heavy, her nipples rising against the cloth.

Still, he did not kiss her.

She inhaled deeply, knowing instinctively that he would not touch her until she made it clear she wanted him to.

Slowly, Prue set her hands on his shoulders, skimming over the fabric of his cape, through his unruly hair, until she cupped both his cheeks in her hands. Stubble covered his jaw and rasped against her thumbs.

"Kiss me," she whispered.

Before she could think, his mouth covered hers, hot and firm and desperate. He tasted of man, of the champagne punch in the ballroom —and something else familiar. The hand that had been curved around her cheek slid beneath her hair to cup the back of her neck, pulling her closer.

Yes. Oh, yes.

Her mind blanked of anything but him, blocking out Whitwell House, the ball, the moonlight. There was only heat, the drumming of her heart, and the taste of him. As he angled the kiss, as his hand skimmed down her back to her waist, she leaned into him.

It had been years since she had been kissed. Seven long years in which she had yearned and dreamed of once again finding love.

Yet it felt like nothing had changed. This kiss was as recognizable as her own heartbeat, as exciting as the fireworks at Vauxhall—and still as seductive as if she had never been kissed before.

"Oh, I say." A disembodied voice echoed out of the darkness. "I do beg your pardon. I had thought the terrace was unoccupied."

Prue raised her head, looked at her lover—for what else was she to call him just now?—and smiled slightly. "Probably an opportune interruption," she murmured.

Without drawing apart, they looked together down the length of the terrace. A man stood just beside the terrace doors wearing a green tunic and green breeches and—Prue frowned. Was that a garland of flowers in his hair?

"Do not laugh, I beg of you." The man turned slightly, revealing a pair of delicate feathered wings. She also noted that he was a rather portly older gentleman, and his belly strained against the tunic. "My wife decided I should play Oberon, King of the Fairies and I thought—well, I did not realize she meant flowers and wings."

"I see." Her lover—she really should find a name for him—cleared his throat, but she felt his chest shaking with laughter. "Is your wife, perhaps, one of the many Titanias in the ballroom?"

"Aye, in a matching green gown—though the flowers and wings look rather fetching on her." Oberon sighed disgustedly. "But one does not cross one's wife, you know. Not when it comes to what she has declared will be the crush of the season—which is why I am here on the terrace. A bit of fresh air, aye? Before I brave the ballroom again and my wife drags me about in this ridiculous costume. At least the refreshments are decent," he added, patting his belly.

"That is something," Prue said, then bit the inside of her cheek to stop her laughter and looked up at her lover.

"Perhaps we ought to remove ourselves to the garden and let Oberon have his moment of peace," he said, mouth curving up slightly.

"I could not agree more."

Four

Her heart was still thudding in her chest, her lips still warm from his, but they stood feet apart as they walked along the gravel path toward—well, she did not know. Somewhere in the extensive Whitwell gardens.

Despite the short distance between them, she felt his presence as if he were still touching her.

Though the London sounds of clopping hooves, carriage wheels, and the calls of coachmen could still be heard, as could the very faint sounds of violins from the ballroom, Prue felt they were very much alone in the gardens. Nothing but moonlight, flowers, and the burble of an unseen fountain surrounded them.

She wanted to kiss this masked stranger again, but somehow knew the moment was lost.

For now. She was not yet done with her mysterious lover.

"You called me warrior in the ballroom." Prue looked up into the night sky, where stars dotted a blanket of deepest black and the moon shown brilliant over the lush gardens. "Perhaps I am, if you mean struggling against the restraints of the *ton*. But what of you? With no recognizable costume, you have no name. What do I call you?"

"I suppose you can choose my name, then, as I chose yours," came his murmured response through the dark. Prue glanced over and visually traced the line of his jaw, the outline of the mask, and broad shoulders still covered in the cape. "As the theme is *A Midsummer Night's Eve*, who shall I be?" he asked.

"Certainly not Oberon." She ruled that character out immediately. This man, in his black cape, mask, and with the edge of danger surrounding him, would never be Oberon. "You are no king of fairies in that boring costume. Even our new friend on the terrace has you beat there."

"Not Bottom, either," he added. In the bright moonlight, she saw him turn his gaze her way, as if gauging her mood. "We have already discovered our papier-mache donkey."

She pursed her lips, trying not to smile. "Are you not an ass, then?"

"I shall leave that for you decide." His shrugged easily, as if he did not care what her position was on the subject. "What should you like to call me?"

"Hm. Well, you have already admitted you have a title. Are you a duke? I could call you Theseus, Duke of Athens, if we are to pretend it is Midsummer's Eve."

"There are a dozen Theseus' in the ballroom as it is, just as there are a dozen Titanias and Oberons—and you, my fair warrior, are fishing for my title to discover my identity." He paused and for a moment there was nothing but the crunch of gravel beneath their feet. "But no, I am not a duke."

"That is something. Most dukes are insufferable." Prue said it without pausing to think and immediately wished to take the words back. This was precisely why she was on the shelf.

"I suppose it is a good thing I am not a duke, then." He clasped his hands behind his back as they continued to walk and seemed entirely unoffended.

"Well, I cannot call you Lysander or Demetrius from the play—I find them both weak, truth to tell."

"Do you?" He sounded intrigued.

"They are quite fluid in their affections. First, they both love Hermia, then they both love Helena, then it all goes awry."

"Due to the fairies' interference," he countered.

"Still, I believe you have more character than Lysander and Demetrius—but I cannot think of a suitable role for you. Not the carpenter or joiner or tailor that put on the play at the end of the—well, play."

"Shakespeare does have a certain sense of humor, does he not?"

"Agreed. I quite enjoy his insults. 'O me! you juggler, you canker blossom, you thief of love!' Can you imagine calling someone a canker blossom?" Prue paused in her step and narrowed her eyes. "Come to think on it, I do believe I've had the dubious pleasure of knowing a canker blossom."

"Is that so?" he asked drily. "I hope it is not me."

"That remains to be seen, for now, but the canker blossom is gone from my life." Seven years gone from her life, along with his broken promises. At least she was having her Season of Scandal before she officially retired to spinsterhood. "Still, that does not resolve what I should call you. Certainly not Puck. Though he is quite a mischievous fairy, I do not think he is handsome enough."

"You think I am handsome?" She did not need to see his face to know his brows were raised in satisfaction.

"Do not be an ass," she answered. "If you were not at least somewhat handsome, I would not have kissed you—that does not mean you should let it go to your head."

"Truth followed by candor." He bowed and gestured for her to move in front of him as they came to a narrow place between the hedgerows.

"'The honour of a maid is her name; and no legacy is so rich as honesty,'" Prue quoted as she passed by him. They were close enough she could feel the heat of him through her uniform, smell the sandalwood of his cologne.

"Now *you* are quoting from the wrong play, my warrior." He stepped once more beside her and they continued through the gardens. "I believe that is from *All's Well That Ends Well*."

"So it is." They turned around a bend in the path and found the source of the burbling water. A fountain speared up into the air, sending out a spray of mist. Prue lifted her face to the light moisture. Though it was only a warm spring evening, the mist was refreshing against her skin. "But let us return to the problem of what to call you. Not Egeus." She slid her gaze his way. "If ever there were an ass, Egeus would be it."

"Because he would not allow his daughter to marry for love?"

"Quite," she agreed emphatically. Deciding to take advantage of her lack of skirts, Prue jumped up onto the circular stone wall surrounding the fountain. Wearing boots, she decided, made her perch quite less precarious than if she wore heeled slippers.

"Does your father believe you should marry for love, then?" her companion asked, standing on the ground below and looking up at her. The spring breeze caught the edge of his cape, making him appear a dashing figure indeed. "Is that why you are on the shelf? You have not found a man you could love?"

"I am on the shelf because I am not good at observing the niceties." She grinned at him. "Look at me now, standing most improperly on the edge of a fountain simply because I can."

Prue extended her arms for balance and began to circle the fountain, walking along the stone wall. Her lover kept pace with her on the ground below, his boots crunching on the gravel pathway while the breeze played with his cape and the unruly ends of his hair.

"I see your point." He looked up into the sky and took a deep breath. "I suppose we are, to some extent, a pair. I have no desire to follow Society's dictates any more than you. Nor am I accustomed to the ballrooms of the *ton*."

"They are admittedly boring after a number of years, though masquerades are always amusing—one never knows whom one is conversing with." Prue looked over at him, but he was still busy looking up into the sky. "Which has me wondering why you are not accustomed to ballrooms."

There was a long pause as she continued her path around the fountain, with only the sound of water and his footsteps filling the night air.

"Until recently, I was a soldier," he said finally. "Now I am not."

"I see." A soldier. Of course, he was. Why was it she was destined to find soldiers attractive? Then again, she was costumed as one. "Now you are a part of Society again and everything is different," she guessed.

"It is not an easy transition from the battlefield to the ballroom."

His tone was unemotional and controlled, and she wondered what else lay beneath the surface.

"I suppose not." Prue jumped down from the edge of the fountain. She wanted more information. She had long since ceased to hope the boy she had loved would return for her, had long since stopped loving him—or trying to—but here was someone she could ask questions of. "What was it like? Soldiering?"

"Bloody cold. And often wet," he answered with a snort. "Begging your pardon."

"I imagine it *was* bloody cold at times. A bit of hard language does not offend me, sir. I am a Warrior, remember?" She turned to face him. "And, if you will not tell me your title, what of your rank?"

———

"Captain." He had earned the position, and selling out to return home still rankled, duty or not. "I was a captain in the Foot Guards."

"Then I finally have a name for you, Captain."

Her voice was filled with laughter and he let it penetrate the coldness inside him. He had left home for battle, setting aside love for duty, and returned once more because of duty. But duty was a cold companion.

"You are sad," she said softly. Stepping close, she set a hand on his cheek. He turned his face into her palm, accepting the comfort she so freely offered. "Why?"

How had she drawn such emotion out of him so quickly? It was as if she understood something behind his words—no one had seen beneath his mask for years, and yet this woman saw not only beneath the half-mask of his costume, but beneath the rest of him as well.

"I left my men." Why was he speaking? It was the dark, he supposed. The night, the moonlight, the woman who was unlike anyone else in the ballroom beyond. "I left my men with a captain they did not trust just before a battle because my brother died. Suddenly I was the—" Noah stopped, unable to reveal to more.

It had been a long time since he had been close to any woman, and they were strangers, no matter what desire flowed between them.

"You do not need to reveal your family title, Captain." She rubbed her thumb over his jaw once, twice, before her hand dropped away.

"Suddenly I was no longer a second son, but a man with land and titles and dependents—and without an older brother." The loss of his brother had been so much worse than leaving the military, but selling out his commission had been nearly as bad a blow.

"I am so sorry." The wind rustled the leaves about them, lifted the ends of her loose hair. She tipped her face up toward his, and he wished once again he could see beyond her mask. "But I understand. You were hurting in multiple ways."

"I never intended to have, never *wanted* to have, the title. Yet here I am." He stepped back, gesturing to his costume. "I am wearing a cape and mask at a *ton* masquerade, sporting a title, and allegedly a great catch on the Marriage Mart."

"'Tis a good thing you are masked, then, or you would be truly miserable tonight." She stepped back as well, and he sensed it was both literal and emotional. When she spoke again, her voice as filled with deliberate light amusement. "The debutantes and mamas would be adamant in chasing you. You would be swarmed by fairies and sprites and Titanias."

"That it is exactly it," he snorted, trying to keep the edge of anger from his voice. "As a captain, I knew my duty and I did it well. As a..." he paused so as not to give away his identity. "A titled peer, I am quite out of my element."

"I understand." His warrior dropped onto the ridge of the stone fountain and gripped the edge of it. He sat beside her, their thighs brushing. He caught her scent again, and the underlying scent of woman began to stir his blood once more. "I am no longer a debutante," she said, "Nor do I want to be. I am a free woman in that I have my own funds, I have reached my majority, and I plan to do whatever I please. Still, I am out of my element this Season as well—particularly as my mother is still hoping for a match."

"I asked you about your father before, and you did not answer if he thought you should marry for love." Noah turned to study her face in the moonlight. Her expression was caught somewhere between a casual mask and resigned acceptance.

"My father does not care whether I marry for love or not." She shrugged, as if dismissing her father as well as love. "My father is a scholar. He writes papers, studies the night sky, observes phenomenon through microscopes, attends lectures with other scientists. He does not have time to worry about his only child."

"I am sorry for it." Lord knew Noah's relationship with his own father had been complicated. That relationship was what had cost Noah love and sent him into the military.

"'Tis nothing. My father taught me a great deal. For example, did you know that about ten years ago, the Royal Society published a catalogue in its *Philosophical Transactions of the Royal Society* of 500 new nebulae? It was published by William Herschel, though I have long suspected it was his sister Caroline who wrote the paper. Still, can you imagine 500 nebulae?" She waved up toward the sky. "And how many more have been discovered since? It has been over a decade since that publication."

"Nebulae?" Her mind would be a fascinating place to explore. "I confess am not certain what that is."

"'Tis a group of stars, sometimes. Or a cloud of some type in the night sky that from Earth appears to be a star. One needs a telescope to view them properly. My father has a simple one, and when I am finally on my own, I shall buy a better telescope. I want to be able to see— well." She broke off, tipped her face to the night sky. Drawing in a long breath, she closed her eyes, as if what she saw was too lovely to view, then sighed deeply. "'There are more things in heaven and earth, Horatio, than are dreamt of in your philosophy.'"

"You are mixing your Shakespeare again." Moonlight caught in the faint dusting of mist that dotted her dark hair, catching the light like diamonds. He reached for one of the long, thick locks and began to twine it about his fingers. She was beautiful, even if he could not see her face. "You quoted Hamlet this time."

"I did warn you I was a bluestocking." Opening her eyes, she turned her head to look at him, the long, dark waves of hair shifting once more over her shoulders and back. A small, knowing smile curved her lips. He could not see her dimple and he wished he could. "Do not think it is your command of Shakespeare that entices me, Captain."

"Heavens, no." Her hair was like silk against his fingers. "I am handsome, too, as you may recall," he grinned at her. "At least more handsome than Puck the fairy."

"Remember, this is my Season of Scandal, Captain." She leaned forward so their faces were close together, their mouths level. Oh, her lips were full, the shape of her jaw delicate. "What is between us is nothing more than a dalliance at a masquerade."

"I do not wear a papier-mache donkey head nor a garland of flowers." He brought his mouth a breath away from hers and fought against the instinct to simply ravish her lips. "Am I suitable for a dalliance, my warrior?

"You are most suitable, Captain," she whispered. "And I intend to take my fill."

They understood each other then. Tonight, one evening nearing midsummer, and no more. He crushed his mouth against hers, tasting that unique flavor of woman that was hers alone. Tart and mysterious all at once.

Noah slipped his hand around her waist to bring her closer yet, sliding her toward him on the edge of the fountain. He wanted her as close as their clothing would allow them to be.

He was drowning in her.

The taste of her was as glorious as the moonlight, the scent of her as heady as the gardens. Her body pressed against his, every curve soft and sweet. Suddenly desperate, he angled the kiss, pressed his tongue against her lips. They parted for him, accepted him, though there was no submission in her actions. Her tongue tangled with his, seeking, exploring, even as his own did the same. Her hands moved over his chest, beneath the cape and up over his shoulders.

"Only a dalliance," she murmured against his mouth.

"Only a dalliance," he agreed, gripping her waist. She wasn't narrow or thin, but rounded in the most lovely shape. He moved his hands up her torso. He wanted to fill his hands with her breasts and discover the shape of them. He reached for the buttons of her soldier's coat—and found the shoulder belt that crossed between her breasts.

It jolted him, reminding him that there was a loaded pistol between them.

He pulled back, breath harsh, and looked into her masked face.

"I had nearly forgotten about your pistol." He set one forefinger on the strap. Wishing it were her skin he was touching, Noah slid his finger along the strap, down, down. Slowly between her breasts.

Her breath hitched, but he moved no faster. He glided his finger along the leather strap, but he imagined what her skin would feel like beneath the uniform. Soft. Smooth. Her breasts round and full, her stomach curved. When he reached her hip, he fingered the cold, hard butt of the pistol in the holster.

"A loaded pistol is a dangerous item, indeed," he said.

"I assured you before I can use it. Do you not believe me?" There was a slight breathlessness to her words, but temper there as well. "Must I demonstrate?"

"Is that a challenge then?" He nipped at her bottom lip.

She moaned slightly, pressed her mouth hard against his, and drew back.

"Of course, it is a challenge," she answered with a wicked smile.

Five

"I wonder if the *ton* shall hear us in the ballroom." They were near to Whitwell House again, standing among the formal garden beds. The light from the ballroom just barely reached them, as did the voices of the guests.

"Do you care if the *ton* hears us?" The Captain asked drily. His fingers were twined with hers and he disentangled them, running his hands up her waist, anchoring her for another kiss. There was demand and need on his lips, and something else. Something softer. A yearning that echoed in her own soul.

That yearning was more than she could bear, so she shifted away from him.

"It is too late for me now to back away from a challenge." Prue withdrew her pistol from the holster. The weapon was solid and cool in her hand, the butt of the pistol as comforting and familiar as the leather bindings on her father's books. "So I suppose I do not care if the *ton* hears us."

"I did not think so." The Captain held out his hand for the pistol. Perhaps it was a trick of the moonlight, but she imagined his hand was roughened with callouses rather than soft and manicured. "May I?" he asked.

"I assure you, it is properly loaded." Prue carefully handed him the double-barrel pistol. It was her father's, though he would be buried enough in his books that evening he would never notice it was missing. She had started borrowing his pistols when she was barely thirteen for target practice and he had yet to speak of it.

"Having known you a few hours now, I do not doubt it is loaded properly." The Captain joggled the pistol in his wide palm, as if gauging the weight of it. Then he brought his arm up, quicker than she could blink, and aimed at something off in the darkness, sighting down the barrel and smiling faintly. He returned the weapon to her, barrels pointed down. "Very nice."

"If one is going to do something, one should do it right," she answered, accepting the pistol.

"The weapon you have brought is quite right—though I still expect you to prove you can use it." He frowned, looking up at the sky. "It is dark, even with the moonlight. Accuracy shall be difficult."

"If you can sight the pistol in this light, then there is enough light for me to shoot." Irritated, Prue rolled her shoulders, then her head from side to side. "Very well, what would you have me shoot to prove my skill? Or do you not believe I am competent."

"I cannot begin to guess." She heard the amusement in his voice and it irritated her further. "You tell me what you think you can shoot."

"I can hit anything you specify within at least ten yards." Prue bit out. "And I shall try very hard not to shoot another guest—including you."

"I shall not doubt you any further, then." He held up his hands in surrender and laughed, damn him. "Very well, that branch." He pointed to a sturdy English oak barely twenty paces away. "It is thick and large enough that it should be a good target even in this moonlight."

So he didn't think she was capable? Well, they would see about that.

Instead of arguing about his suggested target, she lifted the weapon, tilted her head to one side, sighted down the barrel, and closed her right eye.

Then she chose her own target.

Steady. Steady.

The sound of the shot was harsh, the flash of burning powder bright against the dark and the silvery moonlight. Sulfur scented the air.

"You missed." Beside her, the Captain's voice was quite, quite dry.

"I did not miss. I hit precisely the branch I meant to, and I shall do so again." Prue tried not to sound smug, but she knew she did. It was one of her failings. "I aimed for the branch a few feet above your intended target. It is narrower and therefore more difficult. Why should I take the easy shot?"

Without waiting for an answer, she raised her arm, sighted once more, and pulled the trigger. A narrow piece of branch at least two feet long splintered and flew into the darkness.

"Do I pass muster, Captain?" She really ought to learn to control her self-satisfaction, or at least how to keep it out of her voice.

"'Though she be but little, she is fierce.'" His brows rose above his half-mask. "I should say you are more than competent. Where did you learn to shoot with such skill?"

"A long time ago, as a girl. A boy who lived nearby taught me." The boy who had promised to marry her and then had left her. She settled the now-empty pistol back into the holster. "I've never been good at being a proper lady, and I did not want to be left behind embroidering when I could be grouse hunting."

"With your aim, His Majesty's army could use your skill on the battlefield." They began to walk again, and somehow, without speaking of it, they did not approach Whitwell House, but stayed in the gardens. The lilting strains of a waltz floated from the open terrace doors, but they continued to meander through the garden, between rows of meticulous flower beds and trimmed hedges.

If Prue were honest with herself, she did not want to go back to the ball. She wanted more time with her captain.

"What of the boy?" the Captain asked finally. "The one who taught you to shoot?"

"He is the canker blossom I spoke of before—quite gone from my life." With an explanation that had torn her heart in two.

"You sound angry." The Captain's shoulder brushed against hers as they walked, sending little shivers along her skin

"It is best he is gone." Oh, yes, she was angry. In fact, she was surprised at how much anger she still harbored. But then, she had loved him for nearly her entire life—had waited for him for entirely too long. "Childhood love does not stand the test of time, does it?"

"It likely does not." The Captain sounded thoughtful. "Though at the time, it seems it must last forever, does it not? As if there is nothing more important than that childhood love."

A flash of gold caught her eye and set her hand on the Captain's arm. "Look," she murmured, nodding to a small clearing not far away.

Two figures waltzed in the moonlight in a graceful dance. The woman's gown sparkled gold, as did the fairy wings she wore. The man was large and towered above her, and yet he held her so gently the gesture made Prue sigh.

The couple had yet to notice them, they were so intent on each other.

"Let us not disturb them," Prue whispered. "Let them have their stolen moments tonight as well, before we must all wake from tonight's dream."

The Captain's hand slid down her arm, his fingers twining with hers in a movement so natural she did not question it. She had been right that his skin was callused rather than soft—but he would have wielded weapons in battle. Sabre and pistol, perhaps a rifle.

He led her back the way they had come, away from the waltzing couple, his hand warm and strong in hers.

"Have you been in love, Captain?" She tilted her head to look up at him. The light from Whitwell House showed his face in relief. His nose was straight and strong in profile, his jaw sharp-edged. Beneath the mask, he *must* be handsome.

"Once," he said softly. As they passed a peony plant, he broke off one of the blooms and handed it to Prue. "A very long time ago."

"What happened?" She held the blossom to her mouth, ran the soft petals over her lips. They passed a wrought-iron bench surrounded by hedgerows and flowers, and she caught the scents of sweet spring blossoms.

"Duty interfered." He began to walk again, though his shoulders had tensed beneath the cape. "Unfortunately, I hurt her, which I have always regretted. But much like yourself, we were young and foolish. It was not destined to be."

"Youth does not always equate to foolishness." Though perhaps it had been foolish of her to love so fiercely. "Why is it that men put duty above all else?" Prue twirled the peony in her hand and inhaled its scent.

"I suppose because if we do not, we are not considered honorable gentleman."

"Though it is not precisely honorable for you to be kissing an unmarried lady in the gardens." Amused at them both, she tucked the peony into the ties of her mask so it was behind her ear.

"You did say it was your Season of Scandal," he said in a low voice, bringing her hand up to his lips for a light kiss. "And honor can be relative. Sometimes, when you are on the battlefield, honor is all you have."

"It must be difficult, being at war."

"Sometimes, very difficult. And others—it is just life. I had not wanted to accept the commission, but I eventually became accustomed to it. Then, it was time to sell out." He sighed deeply, and once again she heard pain in his voice. "I left my entire company in the command of a man with no training. Both my second in commands were killed in combat, and I left my men with a boy that had never been on the battlefield."

"Oh, God." She knew nothing of war, but she knew enough of life to know what that meant. Commanders—captains—needed experience to both command their men and keep them safe.

"He was green as grass, his commission purchased by his grandfather. Though he was bright and eager, he knew nothing of battle and hardship." The Captain scrubbed his free hand over his face. "Yet I had no choice."

"I suppose you made the choice you had to. 'I do perceive here a divided duty.'" She felt his body relax slightly. "That is *Othello*, not *A Midsummer Night's Dream*."

"How is it you understand?" His voice had eased as well, and that easing helped her own heart.

"Because I may not understand war, but I do understand people. A scientist—an observer—recognizes patterns. The men you trained? The men you led? They will remember what you taught them. Your men learned from you because you were a good leader."

"How can you say that? You've known me all of a few hours—and certainly have never seen me on the field." They were drawing once more near Whitwell house, yet still they did not approach the steps to the terrace.

"Because I am listening to you now, and your dedication is clear. Good leaders care for those they lead." She squeezed his fingers, just the lightest pressure so he would know she spoke the truth. "The new captain will learn from your men and from his own hard experience— but that experience will be supported by the men you commanded."

"'How far that little candle throws his beam', eh?" Self-ridicule all but rode the edge of his words.

"Don't be absurd. You will have made an impact—and that is from *The Merchant of Venice*, by the way. We seem to be straying from tonight's theme." But she felt his pain, strangely as if it were her own. Turning to him, she slipped her arms beneath his cape, wrapped them around his waist and pulled him close. "'There is not one wise man among twenty that will praise himself.'"

Six

"Much Ado About Nothing again, so we are still off the theme." Noah looked down into a face hidden from him behind the white mask, but the light from the windows of Whitwell House were reflected in her eyes. "Why is it that the dark so often reveals more than it conceals?" he murmured. "I've not talked of my men since I have been home, nor have I talked of love. Why I am speaking of them to you, do you suppose?"

"Because it is a masquerade." Her lips curved up and her arms tightened about his waist.

Noah slid his hands over her hips to the small of her back and began to run his fingers up and down her spine. He wished he could feel her skin rather than the coarse wool of her coat. "Because we are not ourselves, are we? 'Mine own and not mine own,' as Helena would have said. We have an opportunity to be someone different, to say things we would not ordinarily say to those close to us."

"'Conceal me for what I am, and be my aid...'" she murmured.

"*Twelfth Night*, I believe?"

"Oh, we are ridiculous, quoting Shakespeare at length. We have spoken real words between us this night, and I want to continue before the night is over. Before this dream is over." Tipping her face up, she laid her mouth on his. Softly, but with a heat that stirred his blood. The peony blossom behind her ear emitted a scent as intoxicating as her own. Noah fought not to take more from her, fought not to deepen the kiss and pull her closer when she leaned away from him. "Tomorrow we shall go our separate ways," she said. "The masquerade will be over."

"And you shall move on to your next scandal."

"So I shall, before I retire into full spinsterhood." She smiled up at him, her expression deliberately inviting. "Once this Season is over, once I have given my mother one more attempt at enticing a husband, I can be done with Society. I can live where and how I choose with my inheritance. So I have decided to take my scandals while I can—and I have decided on you."

"What do you desire, my warrior?" Everything in his body strained toward her, but he knew there were boundaries.

"A kiss." Her eyes behind the mask, her voice, the feel of her body against his, told him that would not be the end of it. "Then I want more."

"Be sure of what you want." Lust roared through him, fueling every cell of his body. He could not take her, not as he wanted to, but he wanted so much more than just a kiss. He wanted to touch her. All of her.

"Just a little more," she murmured. "Enough to show me what I have never experienced."

"Then it shall be as you say." Though his hands wanted to rip at her clothing, Noah carefully worked the buckle of the shoulder belt, sliding it away from her body and dropping it to the ground. The empty pistol thudded against the earth, but the sound was barely an echo in Noah's mind.

With the shoulder belt gone, the uniform buttons were free. He began to work them, experience quickening his movements. He spread apart the coat, exposing her breasts beneath thin linen, and was not certain if she sighed in response, or if he did.

He wanted to hurry, to ruck up her shirt and taste her flesh—and yet he wanted to move slowly. To take his time and savor this final moment of the dream. Noah set a finger against her exposed collarbone, gently exploring. The ridge of bone was delicate, a gentle rise above silken skin.

Her lips parted on an indrawn breath, the sound urging him to hurry. But he didn't. She was inexperienced and only wanted to know a little more.

So he would show her. Just a little, before he did something entirely dishonorable.

He traced a line down the linen shirt, between her breasts. Moonlight shone over her body, emphasizing the shape of her nipples against the fabric. When he reached her waist, he slowly pulled the garment from her breeches, revealing first her soft belly, then her breasts.

He had been right when he had first seen her. Her breasts were magnificent. Full and round and—she moaned as he filled his hands with them. Her head fell back, exposing her mouth and throat while her eyes closed behind the mask.

He bent his head to taste first one breast, then the other. If flesh could be sweet, hers was. Sweet and warm and soft like velvet. When her hands gripped his hair and she shuddered beneath him, he did the best he could to hold on to his control.

———

"I want more." Prue arched her back, wanting him to take more of her breasts in his mouth. How could she have known that her nipples could be so sensitive? That just his touch on them would send arousal skittering somewhere low in her belly? "'I know not by what power I am made bold,'" she quoted, "but I know there is more, Captain, and I want it."

"Not everything," he murmured against the hollow between her breasts. "Masked or not, dream or not, you are still a young lady. Even —" She made a sound of protest and he raised his head to look at her through his mask. His jaw had firmed, though his touch was still gentle. "Even if you do not intend to marry, Warrior, even if you intend to live as you choose as a spinster, I would not have you decide to lose your innocence to a stranger at a masquerade. That is a decision only you can make, but you should not make it in a moment like this."

"Honor. Duty." She laughed softly, cupping the back of his neck and pressing her breasts against his chest. Why was it the only two men she had ever felt this attraction to were consumed by honor and duty? "Very well, Captain. Show me what you will, without taking my innocence."

It was as if her words caused an explosion. In him, then in her.

"'Tis convenient I have experience with fall front breeches." He reached for the buttons, moving quickly at first, then slowly as each movement unveiled more of her. Cool air washed over her skin, moment by moment, button by button. It was as if he wanted to prolong the moment, and she found herself straining against his pace. She wanted *more*.

Suddenly the fabric fell away, night air rushing in to cool the heated parts of her core. She wore nothing beneath the breeches and felt a moment's hesitation at being exposed, but it faded quickly as his mouth found hers. He was gentle and she found reassurance in him, yet there was an underlying need that made her blood pound and her body rise to his as desire renewed within her.

"More," she murmured against his mouth. "More."

With a low moan, he grasped her thigh and brought her leg up, wrapping it around his waist. His fingers found her core quickly, and he began to explore her body, the mound and folds now revealed. She sighed as sensation built within her and arched against him. She wanted something she had read about but wasn't sure existed.

He played at her opening, stroking, then putting one finger inside her. She gasped, both at the intrusion and the pleasure, and dropped her head onto his shoulder.

"There is still more." He spoke the words against her temple, one arm pressing her against him while his finger continued to move in and out of her in a rhythm that made her strain against his hand. When he placed a second finger inside her, she moaned aloud. The pace his fingers set built within her, higher and higher, sending her to a plane of sensation that seemed beyond reason.

"More." His single word was filled with a demand she was helpless against. "I want to take you farther."

He took her mouth again, his kiss full of need and lust. He ran a string of kisses over her collarbone before he pushed up her shirt again to take her right breast in his mouth. Laving it, sometimes gentle, some-time hard, he matched the rhythm at her core. His other hand found her left breast and she shuddered, grateful she was leaning against him and her body did not slide to the gravel path.

It was too much.

Too much sensation. Too much need. Too much of the exquisite pleasure building within her.

As she held on to him, anchoring herself to his shoulders and willing her knees to hold her, his thumb pressed against a part of her she'd never known existed.

Everything shattered into something brilliant and bright.

Prue cried out, unable to stop herself as sensation exploded in her body and created stars behind her eyes. He pressed his mouth against hers again, swallowing the sound, but she could do nothing but shudder against his fingers, once, twice, then try to keep her knees from buckling entirely.

He lifted her up, one arm beneath her knees, the other behind her back. She resisted at first, then relaxed and settled as he cradled her in his arms, satiated and satisfied and unsure if she could walk alone.

"'Are you sure that we are awake? It seems to me that yet we sleep, we dream,'" she murmured, allowing her head to fall against his chest.

He said nothing, only kissed her with a fervency she had not expected, as he carried her toward the wrought-iron bench.

"If I'd worn a gown, I'm sure this would make a beautiful picture of your heroics—carrying the maiden. Instead, I am dressed as a soldier." She laughed lightly, a bit nervous and yet still languid from the sensations that had coursed through her. "You know, fall front breeches are quite convenient when one is considering access to interesting body parts. Although," she added, after a moment's thought, "I ought to rebutton my buttons, in the event someone else comes into the gardens."

"'Thou art as wise as thou art beautiful.'" Even as he spoke the words, she felt his chest rumble with laughter. He settled on the bench, Prue still cradled in his arms, and quickly began to work the buttons of her breeches. "Have you experienced what you wanted, then, my Warrior?"

"Yes, and no." She smiled up into his masked face, still languid and relaxed and feeling no need to move. "The useful part of having a preoccupied scholar for a father means one has access to all sorts of materials. I fully understand I received pleasure, but I know you did not."

"It pleasured me to watch you have your release." His voice was low and raw, but she heard the truth in his words.

"I am no fool, Captain." She also knew enough of the world, had heard enough maids gossiping, that she knew it was not always the truth. "Not all men are like you—and I know there is much more than what we just did."

"There is." He paused, fumbled with her buttons, then recovered and finished the final two. "There are some men who do not understand women's bodies, and there are women who do not understand men's bodies. Or their own, for that matter. There is also more—a joining that can be exquisite if two people are of a mind to make it so."

"I am aware of that aspect. As I said, I had access to quite a lot of books. And of course, my mother provided the, well, coordination of such actions." She paused. "In the event I was married, you understand. But she advised me that I should simply bear it in order to have children."

"Hell. It is no wonder most *ton* marriages are miserable if that is the advice women are given." He pressed his forehead to Prue's, then his lips against hers. Even with her body still pulsing from the aftermath of their lovemaking, she felt desire stirring again. "Sexual pleasure is about sharing your bodies, but also your minds. It is about paying attention to what your partner enjoys as much as what you enjoy. If you end up marrying as your mother wants you to, you may never experience that. If you intend to make your life as you choose, you may experience it as you choose."

"I suppose *you've* taken your pleasure," she said drily, sliding from his lap and onto the bench beside him.

"Unfortunately, men are not held to the same standards as women. I have always strived to be honorable, but yes, I do know what it is like to make love with someone."

"The girl you left?" she asked, curious now about his past.

"No, we were young and we—" he paused, his fingers twining once more with hers. She could not say why the gesture warmed her. "We loved each other very much, but we never explored the physical beyond a few kisses. I would not have known enough then to pleasure her, in any case. I learned on the march, being careful to learn the difference between a woman who is only interested in money and prestige, and a woman I can pleasure." He paused, then snorted. "Why are we having this conversation? 'Tis most inappropriate."

"Because I do not intend to enter the next phase of my life without information." Turning to face him, she set her hands on his shoulders. "You introduced me to something I might not have known otherwise. I thank you for it."

"No, my Warrior," he said softly. "Thank you for trusting me with your body."

Seven

The sounds from Whitwell House were unmistakable. Laughter, surprise, delight.

It was midnight.

The unmasking was at hand.

"We could walk away," the Captain murmured, nuzzling her neck. His lips and stubble sent a combination of excitement and residual waves of pleasure through her. "There is no reason for us to know each other's identity."

"I suppose that is true." Prue tipped her head to the side to allow him better access to her skin and reveled in each touch of his mouth. "'Tis only a dalliance, as we said, so there is no reason to go further."

But she wanted more from him. Not just physically, but to know more. She did not quite know how to phrase her needs, so she pushed up from the bench and paced to where her shoulder belt still lay on the ground. She ought not to leave her father's pistol behind.

"I do not want tonight to be the end of things between us." His words were quiet and stopped her fingers as she buckled the belt over her torso. "I understand you don't intend to marry, that you intend to set up your household and live independently as you choose."

Prue looked over at him, still sitting on the bench in his cape and mask.

"It is true I don't intend to continue with the *ton*." But what did she want?

She did not want to suffer the vagaries of the *ton* after six long years of toeing the line. She no longer wanted to be obedient to her mother and father and do what was expected of her. Or to marry because there was no one she cared enough about to concede to, let alone to give up her independence now that she had it.

"I am only here," Prue said slowly, "to appease my mother for one final season before I set up my own household."

But she did want more of *him*. The Captain whose face she did not know. The man who could bring her pleasure. She hoped she could bring him pleasure as well.

"I intend to remain a spinster, yes. A virgin, no. 'But earthlier happy is the rose distilled than that which, withering on the virgin thorn, grows, lives and dies in single blessedness,'" she finally said. "I say we shall make a pact, Captain. We agree to engage in a mutually satisfying affair, until such time as either of us tires of such a union."

"An affair." He stood, the cape swirling about his broad shoulders. "Do you know what you are asking for?"

"Yes. I want to experience lovemaking." Prue tightened the buckle of the shoulder belt. The weight of the pistol at her waist was strengthening. "I want to feel desired, I want physical love, that is all. I am finished with Society and have no reason to continue with it. I want the freedom to choose my own way, and I now have it. Therefore, I want to forge an agreement between us."

"What are your terms?" He strode toward her until they stood close enough that his male scent seemed to surround her.

"When I set up my own household at the end of the Season, I want to continue a relationship with you for as long as we are both interested." Setting her hand on the butt of the pistol, she stared her captain straight in the face and did not look away. "An affair, for as long as we choose."

"I need to marry at some point, in order to do my duty by the title." He breathed deep, the light of Whitwell house shining over his face. "When I marry, I shall not break my vows. I will be true to my wife."

"Understood." Why did she feel like she was bargaining for the rest of her life? "We are agreed to continue this affair for as long as we choose?"

"Yes." His lips curved up. "Shall we seal our bargain with a kiss?"

He cupped her face in his hands, set his lips to hers. She parted for him, let the taste of him settle into her. His mouth was firm, his touch soft. Everything in her body came alight, and she knew that however long their affair lasted, it would be everything she'd hoped for.

"We are agreed, and now it is time for the unmasking." The Captain nodded to the house beyond. "It is happening in there, where everyone can see. Out here in the garden, it is only us. No one need know about our relationship but us two."

He was so close, just inches away, his heat and scent filling her. She reached for the ties of his mask. The ribbons were soft against her fingertips, the ties easy to loosen. Her stomach clutched in anticipation and fear. Who was he? Was the man behind the mask the man she wanted? She had known the men of the *ton* for six years, had watched them attend functions, woo wives, marry, sire children, find lovers when they became discontent.

But she wanted to know him. This man. Her Captain. She wanted to see his face.

Pulling away the half-mask, her heart beating wildly in her chest, she studied his face. Handsome, as she had thought. Thick brows, keenly sharp features. His nose was straight and strong, his lips full and skilled, she knew.

She met his gaze, those deep set cobalt blue eyes, and—

The half-mask fell to the ground, forgotten.

She knew that face. Oh, it had changed in the past seven years, but she knew that face. His features had become leaner, hardened. There was a scar just over his right eyebrow that had not been there before. His jaw was stronger, the stubble thicker than when he'd left her.

But the eyes were the same. She should have known it, should have seen it. The strength, the intensity, even the color. She should have known it was him.

"*Noah.*" Before her mind planned it, her fist connected hard with his belly. His breath exploded out as he bent double, though whether it was with shock or pain, she could not decide. Her fist throbbed, but it was nothing to the ache in her heart.

"What?" Rubbing a hand against his belly, Noah stared her. Confusion on his handsome face. "What?"

She ripped her mask off, heedless of the ribbons and the peony behind her ear, and tossed all of it to the ground.

"*Prue*?" Shock reverberated in his voice, widened those damnable blue eyes.

"You told me you loved me." Furious, years of pain and anger welled up inside her. "Even when you said goodbye, you said you loved me." Prue fumbled for the pistol at her waist, then remembered she had already used both bullets. "Dammit, I am empty of rounds and I did not have the foresight to bring supplies to reload."

"For which I am exceedingly grateful." Noah muttered, taking a step back and holding up his hands in surrender.

"I *waited* for you, Noah. For years." Noah's face, once as familiar to her as her own, was caught between moonlight and the glow of the windows of Whitwell House—just as it was caught somewhere between her memories and the reality before her. "Through the first year, through first few Seasons. I waited and waited, but you never came."

"I made you no promises, Prue." Noah's voice was hard and strong, as it might have been on the battlefield. The face she had known so well was now foreign to her.

"Oh, but you did," she bit out. Why was a breaking heart so painful? "You promised to marry me."

"I had a duty to my family name." His features hardened, the mix of candlelight and moonlight throwing his face into harsh relief.

"Duty." Temper boiled up inside her. She stalked toward him and poked him hard in the chest with her finger. "What of your promise to *me*?"

"I had to make a choice between you and my obligations." His face did not change expression, and she could see how he would have looked commanding his men. "Did you think I wanted to accept the commission?"

"I don't know, Noah. Damnation." Prue wished she had been prepared to face him again. To face the pain he had caused her. "I suppose it was my own fault I expected you to return. I loved you so much." She stared up into the face of a man who was now a stranger to her, which nearly broke her heart again. "'I was enamored of an ass.'"

Eight

Surly from a sleepless night spent thinking of Prue, Noah tugged on the reins of his gelding to guide him through the carriages and carts on Park Lane.

He had given her an explanation when he left for the military. Still, he owed Prue more. He had always known he did. Perhaps it would be better to admit that the explanation he had given had been unworthy of what had been between them.

The fact remained that there was still something between them. Not just their history, but passion as well. The same passion of their youth, yet stronger. Deeper.

Noah dismounted in front of the steps of the Heatherstone townhouse and gestured to one of the numerous street urchins loitering about. The boy scuttled over, and Noah handed him the horse's reins.

"I should not be above a half hour," he said.

That was, of course, if Prue would see him at all.

Noah took the front steps two at a time and gripped the brass handle of the door knocker. Two brisk beats later, the door was opened by a liveried butler.

"May I help you, sir?" He was, much like Noah's own butler, impassive and dour, and completely uncaring of who might be at the door.

"Please tell Miss Prudence Chapman the Earl of Parkwood would like to speak with her." Noah wasn't certain precisely what he would say, but he knew they must talk.

"I am sorry, my lord." The butler did not change his expression. "Miss Chapman has gone out. If you would care to leave a card, I shall inform her of your call."

"When will she return?" Impatient, Noah set his hand on the door, forcing it to remain open. He had not stayed up all night to be turned away now.

"I cannot be certain, my lord." The butler looked at Noah's hand, then back at his face, and raised his brows. "She has just left for a ride in Hyde Park. It may be an hour or more before she returns."

Noah was not surprised. The Prue he had known all those years ago would need space to run out her anger.

After flipping the street urchin a coin, Noah remounted his horse and turned the gelding toward Hyde Park. No doubt he would find Prue in the most open spaces where she could be free.

As he guided the horse into the park, his mind circled around the same facts that had kept him awake all night.

How had he not recognized Prue? All the signs were there. Her father's disinterest and preoccupation with his scholarly pursuits, the 'boy' who taught her to shoot, and the brilliant and restless mind unwilling to accept Society's dictates.

Prue had not changed. She had grown into a questioning, strong woman, just as her body had grown into the full curves her shape had hinted at when she was seventeen.

The essence of her had not changed.

The Prue he had dreamed of in those early years in the Guards was the same now as she had always been. Full of life, determined to go her own way, and smarter than nearly anyone he knew.

When he saw the figure moving at a full gallop across the park on a pretty chestnut mare, dark hair streaming behind her, Noah knew it was Prue.

She had never been afraid of horses. Even now, she didn't control the animal, but moved with it, as completely in harmony as a horse and rider could be. Well off the gravel track, she cut across an open field of Hyde Park, flying over grass still glistening with morning dew.

Heads turned as the thunder of hooves reached other riders moving sedately on the dirt and gravel strip of the Old King's Road. They were taking the morning air, enjoying a quiet ride—and being treated to Miss Prudence Chapman, daughter of Baron Heatherstone, acting anything but dignified.

No, Prue did not fit amongst the *ton*.

But then, neither did he.

Need for her reared up and gripped Noah as he watched her, clutching and clawing at his insides. How could he want this woman so badly, even after all this time? Giving her pleasure last night had been as much torture as denying himself her body when they were young.

Well, they were no longer young.

Noah set off at a gallop after her, moving over grass and rich turf to reach her. Prue had reined in and was giving her mare its head to cool down. As Noah passed the groom trailing her, he nodded his head in greeting—at least Prue had observed *that* propriety.

As the sound of the gelding's hooves alerted her, Prue turned in the saddle to face him. Early spring sunlight shone on her face, brightening her flushed cheeks. The military-style cap emphasized the shape of her deep brown eyes and sharpened the set of her chin. Her hair was loose beneath the cap, once again flowing in deep brown waves about her shoulders and back.

Yet one more instance when Prue went her own way.

"Prue." Noah called out as he drew near. Beneath him, the gelding tossed his head, and though the animal slowed at Noah's physical commands, he moved restlessly against the restrictions.

Noah felt the echo in his own body. He, too, was restless and edgy. Damn if it wasn't Prue's fault.

"Noah?" Recognition flared in her dark eyes and the smile curving her lips died away. "I didn't expect you."

"Clearly not." He slowed and drew his horse alongside hers. "But I owe you an explanation. A better one than I gave you last night, and certainly better than when I left all those years ago."

"What more is there to say?" The mare circled beneath her, intuiting her mistress's unrest. "One day you and I planned to marry. We promised, lying beneath the trees in the orchard of the Grange. Do you not remember?"

He did. A blanket, the warm autumn sun. Ripe apples Prue had picked herself, hiking up her skirts to climb the apple trees—he'd had a wonderful vision of what those legs were capable of.

"I remember, Prue."

"The very next day, you called on me to tell me you were accepting a commission in the military." Her features were carved with a sorrow that made his chest ache. "You *left* me."

"I had a duty to my family." There was so much more, but he found he could not get the words out.

"Duty." She said the word with the same disgust she had used the night before. Her mare circled once more, reacting again to Prue's temper. "I loved you, Noah. I had loved you since I was twelve. When you left, it broke me."

"I loved you as well, Prue." He spoke softly, his voice barely a whisper on the morning air. "I loved you more than my life, but Father gave me no choice."

"You chose duty." Her words were bitter, the deep brown of her eyes filled with temper and unhappiness. "Was there no duty to me and your promises?"

"Prue—"

"Enough." Digging her heels into the mare's sides, Prue escaped in a flurry of hoofbeats and clumps of flying grass.

"Oh, no," Noah muttered. "I'm not done with you yet, Prue."

———

"Miss Chapman is still not at home, my lord." The butler, having opened the door to Baron Heatherstone's townhouse to Noah for the second time in an hour, stared down his nose with complete condescension and, if Noah was not mistaken, animosity as well.

"Bollocks." As he had before, Noah planted his hand on door to keep it open, using all the force of his temper to hold the door in place.

"I followed Prue here from Hyde Park not five minutes ago. She is most certainly at home."

"My lord—" The butler began to wrestle with the door, trying to shut it in Noah's face. "She is *not* at home."

"She might not be available to callers, but she *is* at home." Though the butler was likely twice Noah's age, he was strong enough Noah had to press his full weight against the door.

"Noah, you are entirely annoying." Prue stood in the drawing room doorway just across the entry hall, wrestling with the riding cap pinned to hair. "Oh, let him in," she said to the butler. "Noah Clarke will not stop until he has his way—he always has been a stubborn bastard."

The butler stopped struggling with the door and stepped back, but he narrowed his eyes at Noah. "Very well, Miss Chapman, but I shall be just outside the drawing room should you need me. With a large foot-man. And a pistol."

"Understood," Noah ground out. He moved through the open doorway, strode across the parquet entryway floor and into the drawing room. "Though I'm quite sure Miss Chapman can handle herself."

"Indeed." The butler's reply was cut off by a sharp snap as Noah shut the door behind him.

"There is nothing left to say to each other, Noah." She glared at him over a plush settee as she jerked the pins from her cap. Her hair shifted over her shoulders, ribbons of chocolate sliding over a rich blue riding habit.

"I disagree. There is a great deal of history to be covered."

"I do not care about our history, Noah. It has been seven years since you left, six since I have been on the Marriage Mart." Her cheeks were flushed with anger, her pointed chin lifted high as she met his gaze evenly. "*You* may be in need of a wife and heir, but I am no longer in need of a husband."

I am quite plain beneath this mask, she had said the night before. Perhaps she would not catch the eye of every dandy in a ballroom, but all Noah could see was an inner beauty that shone from her, particularly in temper.

"Even if I were in need of a husband," she continued, spinning away from him. "We were barely children when we promised we would marry —then you made your choice to take the commission."

"Damnation, Prue, I did not *have* a choice," he exploded. Grabbing his hat from his head he tossed it onto the nearest table, knocking over an ornate wooden clock. It clunked as it hit the tabletop, then chimed dully. "My father purchased my commission. I was the second son and expected to do my duty. I did not even know he had purchased it until he presented it to me. When he did, I told him you and I planned to marry and he forbade it—and until we reached our majority, we could not marry without permission. What should I have done? I was only eighteen years old."

"I do not know." Prue stared at him with those deep brown eyes for a long moment. "I remember your father well enough and how harsh he could be—I do not know what you could have done."

"You were but seventeen, Prue." Noah stepped toward her, setting his hands on her upper arms. "You were always the focus of my life. Every day you were there, fishing or riding or just walking. Laughing. Sitting on the old bridge and dangling our feet in the water. Whatever we did, you were there every day, Prue. I loved you more than life itself and I—I was hesitant. You trusted that our future would always be the same. That nothing would change."

"I did trust you. I trusted *us*." She set her hands on this chest, gripping the lapels of his coat. "Looking back, I see those two young lovers, swamped by their passion for each other—and with little knowledge of life and even less power to oppose their parents. Still, you could have sold your commission after a few years. Left the army."

"What would you have had me do? Abandon my men?"

"You abandoned *me*," she spit out. That truth was bitter, and he felt it in his soul. "Was I less important?"

"I don't know, Prue." Noah dropped his hands away from her and scrubbed them over his face. He had not shaved that morning and the stubble along his jaw was thick and rough. His breath came out in a long, unhappy sigh. "You were no less important than my duty, but I was trapped."

She made a strangled sound in her throat, almost as if she were strangling a sob. "And I was left alone."

Nine

"Christ, Prue. I am sorry. I'm so sorry I broke my vow to marry you." He circled his arms around her and this time, Prue had no urge to fight him. As angry and hurt as she was, she needed his touch. He laid his forehead against hers and whispered, "I cannot ask for forgiveness. I do not expect it. I can only ask for understanding."

True regret resonated in his voice and broke open a part of her heart she had locked long ago.

"Damn you, Noah. If you were arrogant or superior, or had not come to call this morning, I could let it go, but you're too...too... decent." Worse, his mouth was so close to hers. She wanted to kiss him, even now. While the commonplace, the easiness of daily life had been their mainstay, there had always had desire between them. "I missed you, Noah. Like a part of my soul was missing."

"I felt the same, but I had no choice. Just as I had no choice in returning home." Noah broke off, grief flashing over his lean features. "My brother died just months ago. The morbid sore throat, of all things. And here I am." She heard his audible swallow. "Now I am the Earl of Parkwood."

Oh, her heart ached for so many reasons. For Noah, for his brother, for their family.

And for herself.

"I am sorry, Noah. I did not know." Noah and his brother had been so close as boys. She had followed them around the Grange, around the woodlands, learning to shoot, to climb trees, to fish. They had never left her out. She had been one of them—and she supposed that experience had forged who she was now. Prue set her hand on Noah's chest. Beneath her fingers, his heart was pounding. "I had not heard of his death. I simply assumed your brother had not come up to London this season."

"He was buried before I returned from the Continent." Noah set his hand over hers. His fingers were warm, and when they twined with hers, she did not stop him. There was still enough between them that she grieved with him. "I loved him, Prue."

"I did as well." Parkwood Grange, the family seat, had been barely a stone's throw from her own childhood home. The three of them had been inseparable, though it had always been Noah she loved. Heart aching, she pulled away from him. "Now you must take your brother's place. Once more, you must do your duty—this time as the earl."

Those brilliant blue eyes stared into hers for a long time, and she found she could not move. It was as if he held her there simply by the intensity of his gaze.

"Prue, there is still something between us." His voice was low, even rough, with emotion. "We proved that last night at the masquerade, even when we did not recognize each other."

"It is much too late for us, Noah." But oh, something in her still yearned for him. She resented it, wanting to send him away after all the years of pain. Yet she couldn't. "It was only lust between us last night. Nothing more."

"Perhaps." He breathed deep and stepped toward her. "But perhaps there was more. I think we owe it to ourselves—to each other—to see if there is more."

Did she dare take a chance with him? Prue realized she was rubbing her chest just above her heart. She might be hurt by him again and she wasn't sure she could live through that again.

"You broke your promises to me, Noah."

"Then I shall make no promises now—except that I shall not run off to war." The wry half-smile on his face was so familiar, so dear, it further broke open that lock around her heart.

Still.

"That is not much of a promise," she snorted.

"I am here to stay, Prue. I am the Earl of Parkwood, ensconced at the family seat and even in the House of Lords. I am not leaving again." He lifted his chin and met her gaze. "A chance, Prue. That is all I want. All I ask. We need to know if it would have been good between us, or if it was only a dream. Otherwise, we shall always wonder."

Prue cocked her head to one side and contemplated him. She was older now, and wiser, but so was Noah. She could protect her heart if needed, and she certainly still wanted him physically.

"I'm independent now, as I said. I can live on my own without a husband. I don't need the *ton* to approve of me, or my mother and father to care for me. I'm of age and then some." She stepped close and framed his face with her hands. "But I suppose that does not mean there is no room for you in my life."

He laughed and pressed his lips to hers. "Would an independent woman such as yourself be willing to entertain a gentleman caller?"

"Perhaps." She tilted her head and met his gaze. "But be forewarned, if you should break a promise again, I will hunt you down with a pistol."

"That is a term I can accept."

Epilogue

Prue studied the little gold flecks that floated through the afternoon sunbeams shining through their bedchamber window. They seemed to be a blessing, somehow. Wishing them good luck.

One year married now. A year in which she had learned who Noah was—different, and yet the same. But so was she, and he had learned those parts of her as well. Somehow, those parts of the children they had been fit together with the adults they had become.

Prue snuggled into the soft bedding, then sighed and turned her head to look at Noah, bathed in that sunlight. He slept peacefully on the pillow beside her, his black hair stark against the white linen. Gold illuminated every feature, the scar above his eye, the long, thick lashes that lay on his cheeks. He breathed evenly, his hand resting on her belly even in sleep.

Did he know? Surely not. Prue was only just certain herself.

And yet.

They had fallen asleep after their lovemaking, and though the sun slanting through the bedchamber window had woken her, she did not want to disturb Noah's slumber.

Once year today. An entire year of lovemaking, laughter, intellectual conversation, and—she was delighted to discover—her participation in the running of his various estates. They even fished on the old bridge from time to time and brought home their own dinner.

The telescope Noah had bought her as a wedding gift sat in the window of the room he had set aside for her own space, along with whatever instruments and books caught her fancy. The matching pistols they commissioned were set aside in the study for whenever they decided on target practice.

Life was never perfect, but for the moment, for just now, it felt perfect.

Prue twined her fingers in Noah's hair, enjoying the silky texture against her fingers. He knew her better than anyone in the world, and always had.

He stirred slightly, his hand curving more possessively over her belly. On a satisfied sigh, he nuzzled his lips against her neck, then unerringly found her mouth for a long, drugging kiss. His afternoon stubble scraped deliciously over her sensitive skin and she found her body stirring once more.

Would she never tire of him?

"'What angel wakes me from my flow'ry bed?'" he murmured. Opening his eyes, he shifted so he could see her face more clearly. His long, lean body gathered her close, his strength against her softness. "Ah, 'tis my beautiful Prue."

He pressed another soft kiss against her lips.

"I suppose it is a good thing you persuaded me to marry you, Noah." Prue curled closer to him. He was everything strong and right, comforting and desirable. "I believe there is more than just the two of us to consider now."

"Hm?" He looked blankly at her, cobalt eyes still vague with sleep. "More than two of us?"

"There are three of us." She set her hand over his, still splayed over her stomach, and smiled softly.

In a heartbeat, Noah sat bolt upright, eyes wide with shock.

"Are you certain?" His hair stood on end from her fingers moving through it, his jaw unshaven today as she liked it best. And oh, those brilliant eyes called to her.

"Aye. There is no doubt," she laughed and stretched against the soft bed linens. "I've not had the physician in yet, but I've missed my courses twice."

Noah turned his hand palm up and twined her fingers with his. It was a connection that always brought them closer. She knew he felt it as well when his face softened.

"I cannot tell," he murmured, peering closely at her, at her belly.

"It's too early, you idiot." She laughed. "You won't see a swell for at least a few months yet."

"But you are certain?" He lay down beside her, propping his head in his hand so he could look down at her.

"Yes." Everything in her warmed as he dropped a kiss lightly on her lips. "You are a father."

"It seems a thousand years ago we sat on the old bridge, side by side, pulling up trout." He spoke softly, lean body still pressed against hers, but with all his focus on her face. "It seems a hundred years ago we met again at the masquerade. But do you know, even those thousand and hundred years seem like only a dream compared to what we have now."

"Noah."

"I love you, Prue. I always have. If I had been older or stronger, things might have been different." He smiled though, brilliantly. "Yet I would not change a thing. We may have missed a few years, but I daresay we are the better for it."

"I suppose you are right. Had I not been ready for scandal, perhaps none of this would come to be."

"I promise, Prue, that I shall care for you both." His hand moved over her belly, even as he mouth met hers with all the love and desire that had pulsed between them since the beginning.

"Always."

THE END

Despite being a native Michigander, **ALYSSA ALEXANDER** is pretty certain she belongs somewhere sunny. And tropical. Where drinks are served with little paper umbrellas. But until she moves to those white, sandy beaches, she survives the cold Michigan winters by penning romance novels that always include a bit of adventure. She lives with her own set of heroes, aka an ever-patient husband who doesn't mind using a laundry basket for a closet and a small boy who wears knight-in-shining-armor costumes for such tasks as scrubbing potatoes.

Visit her online at www.alyssa-alexander.com, https://facebook.com/AlyssaAlexanderAuthor, and https://twitter.com/alexanderalyssa.

www.ingramcontent.com/pod-product-compliance
Lightning Source LLC
Chambersburg PA
CBHW051852130726
47987CB00002B/793